The Red Eye

A. Akinosho

Contents

One

Ciara

I woke up later than usual today but that didn't stop me from feeling energized, ecstatic, and excited. My three E's, I call them. Nothing can ruin the three E's for me today. I could almost feel the sea breeze, my feet in the warm sandy beach, and sun hitting my bikini-clad body; boy did I work hard to fit in that itsy-bitsy bikini, and the plan is to savor every minute with Kevin on the sandy beach, soaking in the sun and sipping Margaritas.

The sounds of pantyhose ripping brought my daydream to a screeching halt as I briskly moved to my desk carrying my laptop and coffee. I'm presenting my interior design ideas for the upscale exclusive club today. A ripped panty hose is not welcomed right now. Just another thing trying to ruin my three E's, not today.

In my energized and ecstatic state, I'd tried to rush through my daily routine causing a coffee spill on my white blouse, and with no time to change, I covered the mess with a jacket.

Of course, my hair also tested my happiness today, I'd stared at a picture-perfect bad hair day this morning and I did the best I could with cream, oil, and a good brush. Even I know it won't last.

I took the pantyhose off as soon as possible and changed my heels to ballet flats, hoping no one would notice my unshaven legs. Yes, unshaven legs without pantyhose. Gross. I blame that on my girls making me party till late last night.

My design presentation was almost a bust, no thanks to that Hillary bitch that's always trying to steal my ideas and color schemes and tries to present them as hers.

Now frizzes, I can feel you between my fingers and the weird stares from my colleagues. Calling this a bad day is an understatement, but nothing can steal my joy because I'm on the E-steroid today!

After my presentation, I asked my boss Mary if I could leave early today since I had a trip planned. She was kind enough to let me leave once I tied up all loose ends. After finishing my task, I decided to drive over to Kevin's instead of waiting for him at my place. I'd already stowed my travel bag in my car before my outing with my girlfriend last night. Given how my day was unfolding, it was a smart move.

Kevin had texted me saying he would be at the office till 3 p.m., I figured I could wait for him at his place and maybe shave my legs while I wait for him.

Kevin and I would be lazy bees in the sun of Mexico by this time tomorrow. We need this trip, or should I say, I really need this trip. Not only to relax, but also as a last-ditch effort in saving our four years' relationship. We started dating during our second year of college, stayed together for two years, then broke up just before graduation. He'd said he needed more space, and that I was not giving him that.

After graduation, I moved back home. Months later, still unable to find a job, my sister suggested I broaden my horizons, so I started applying for jobs in different states. Finally, Los Angeles, California, gave me the offer and opportunity I couldn't refuse. Moving to LA was difficult for me because I'm very close with my family, and making new friends wasn't an elementary thing for me either. However, I connected with a girl at work named Amy. She was an all-time Californian girl, which was great because she knew all the best places in town.

One afternoon, during lunch, we saw Claire, a woman from the finance department. She had just walked out of the bathroom with toilet paper stuck to her heel, and Amy was kind enough to immediately get her attention. The next day, Claire saw us having lunch and asked to join us. From then on, we became the three musketeers. Claire had moved to LA from New York. She's really on the wild side, but I love her for it. Whenever I miss my family, I have these lovely ladies to comfort me.

A year into my life in LA, with no boyfriend on the radar, my disdain for online dating, and Claire repeatedly saying, "If you don't go online, you must out," so there I was, partying with my friends when Kevin walked up to me. I was surprised to see him; I had no idea he lived in LA. He seemed calmer and more in control. I was glad to see him. He asked for a date, and we started dating again. Initially, we were inseparable.

Now, two years later, I'm running extra miles to stay in the relationship. We are at the point where we both like to say we are in a relationship just so we can say we are not single.

I can't remember when we last had sex, considering we agreed to have a baby. We make plans for outings and somehow found ways to cancel at the last minute. My friends don't like him, and I can barely tolerate his friends. Honestly, this Mexico trip is our Hail Mary. Fingers crossed, we might get back on track and salvage this relationship.

My friends keep telling me I should break up with him. Steven, my best friend since kindergarten, can't stand Kevin. My mom is clear about him not being the one for me. There's just something about him they all don't like.

Who knows, maybe the drinking or that obnoxious mouth of his? But I tell myself we are great together, every relationship has its funk, and this period is just our funk, though my subconscious sometimes reminds me that I'm overcompensating. Honestly, he always made me laugh, and that, to me, is important. He's very good with money, too. God knows there are too many broke guys out there that try to paint the picture of having it all.

We've tried unsuccessfully to get pregnant, but we were eventually told by my doctor that I couldn't have kids. The news shattered me, but Kevin said not to worry, and that we could always adopt or go the surrogate route. His support was unwavering. Maybe that was the reason I didn't listen to my friends whenever they told me to break things off with him.

Hopefully, a warm sandy beach will magically cleanse our funk. I figured I would get a better perspective on why I kept trying to save this relationship, and possibly where we were headed by the time, we return in ten days.

As I drove to Kevin's place, I realized that though my day started somewhat messy, I'm still on my three-E steroid: energized, ecstatic, and excited, and so looking forward to my bikini-clad moments with endless margaritas.

I arrive at his place and use my key to unlock the door. The sound of a woman moaning is the first thing I hear. At first, I think it is the TV, but the TV is showing jeopardy and it's muted; my feet seem to move without my command towards the moaning sound, my suspicions were confirmed—Kevin's head bobbed up and down between the thighs of a buxom blonde. His tanned butt, that I always thought was sexy, now looks ridiculous.

A feeling of repulsion washed over me as I stared at their exposed form. I stand watching the live amateur porn. He's feasting on her like a starved dog. This is a perfect fight, flight, or freeze moment. I should fight like any angered girlfriend, but I freeze because shock and disbelief are still having a tango in my head thus, I freeze in the moment. I let out a weighed sigh because I don't have any more fight left in me for him. The stars of the moment finally sense my presence, and they turn to me.

"Shit!!! I'm sorry Ciara, this isn't what it looks like," he says as he rushed to cover himself and I burst out laughing.

"Finish up, Kevin, and enjoy it because we are certainly over." Good thing I went off plan and we haven't boarded our flight. I stormed out of there and ran back to my car. I couldn't think of where to go or what to do. I get on the highway driving with no destination in mind. I let out a loud scream and turned the radio on and right there, the song "Since You Been Gone" by Kelly Clarkson came on. I'm driving, singing, and screaming like a madwoman. I finally let go of the rope I've been clinging onto; my heart should be shattered, but it's relieved of the binding chains in a strangled relationship. The shackles are broken and I'm free. Within me, they shatter and fall to the ground as my three E's bubbles popped; they were all illusions anyway.

Oh! What A Day in the Life of Ciara.

I drove aimlessly, thinking maybe I should head to the airport and head to Mexico alone. I would like to call

Amy, but I don't want her to say, "I told you so," or "Good for you." Not sure what I want right now. My phone rings, knocking me out of my aimless wandering thoughts. The caller ID shows my mom.

"Hi, Mom."

"Ciara, dear, where are you?"

"Driving, Mom."

"I have some bad news. Nana had a heart attack. She's in the hospital."

Could this day be any worse? I should scream till my lungs explode today.

"Is Grandma going to be, ok?" I calmly asked though my mind was screaming.

"We don't know yet. We're all here at the hospital. Just wanted to let you know before you head to Mexico," she says.

"I'm not going to Mexico anymore. Kevin and I broke up," I blurt.

"Oh, I am sorry dear, are you alright?"

"I couldn't be better, mom. I have 10 days of vacation; I'm coming home."

"Alright dear, we will be expecting you." Just like that, I had clarity. I'm heading home to my family that I love.

I exit the freeway and direct myself towards the air-port. After a lengthy discussion, I finally earned my seat on the red-eye flight by redeeming everything in my points account and paying an additional amount for a first-class ticket that was way out of my budget. But I needed to get out of LA like yesterday. I didn't care. I grabbed a change of clothes from my bag and checked my luggage in.

After changing, I tame my frizzy hair. I patiently wait for my late flight to Chicago. My thoughts wander to the last two years with Kevin. The signs of him cheating and our romance cracking every day were right there in plain sight. I just didn't want to let go. I knew deep down I was no longer in love with him, but my baby fever and his support had clouded my judgment. Now, I had wasted a total of four years of my life with him. I inhaled and exhaled, hoping to relieve my pain. "Better late than never," I mantra; my consolation words.

I finally relax, I would have to borrow clothes from my sister; all my bikinis and skimpy outfits that I planned to wear in Mexico would not work in Chicago's January weather.

Two

PHILIP

Why am I the one that has to fly to Chicago to resolve this issue? I tried for the umpteenth time to convince my dad to send Henry, but he insisted that I get on the plane, and that my showing up was a better representation of our commitment to the management and staff.

The worst part, I had to leave immediately and take the red-eye flight out since dad had to take the private jet. Private charters were fully booked to Chicago, which is crazy, why is anyone flying to that freezing location? I can't remember when last I flew commercial, unfortunately, I must, today. Once management got organized and operations back on track, I'll leave Chicago with plans to send Henry back and certainly before the winter is over. Should be a good payback for him.

The thought of the cold Chicago weather has my mind freezing before I leave LA. I'm not happy about this trip at all. I had plans with some ladies this weekend which I had to nix. Henry, my best friend since college, who also works for my dad's company, had a great time laughing at me about my nixed dates.

My phone ringing interrupts my thoughts.

"Hi honey, did you get my message?" Hillary's squeaky voice pierces my eardrums. Why does she always sound like a scratched turntable?

"Yes, I did," I mumble back.

"Phil, are you sure you must travel to Chicago? Can't Henry go?"

"No, he can't, I have to be there, I promise to be back in time for your friend's wedding," I state matter of fact to assure her. Though, giving the change, I would rather miss the wedding. Guess, I still prefer Hillary to the harsh Chicago winter.

"Ok, call me when you get to Chicago."

"Will do."

I breathed relief the moment I hung up. Hillary and I had been dating for about five years and I know I can't marry her though she is convinced we are heading down the aisle. Our families are friends, and my mother has the wedding date and planner all set, but I know that it's a date that will never happen. The families keep pitching us together, making it hard to break things off with her.

Hillary fits the perfect wife symbol and social class, but marriage with her would be rolling in the same circle.

Nothing new, no excitement. We barely have much to say to each other than to discuss social outings. Sex with her is no longer exciting. I have sown my unroyal wild oats as much as possible. She acts oblivious to the fact that I cheat on her all the time. All she sees is her name as Mrs. Webster, not if we are compatible. I think she's convinced herself that once I marry her, I'll suddenly stop seeing all the other women. Not going to ever happen. I'm a player for life. Why the hell would I want to give that up? I'm not the marrying kind, I know it and she knows it too but refuses to accept.

I know a lot is missing with us, but I can't place my finger on anything specific that I can use as a perfect reason to break up with her. We have been together too long; the relationship feels more like we are accommodating each other rather than two people that should be in love and want to spend their lives together.

I looked around the crowded airport lounge, trying to distract myself from the thought of the complicated re-lationship I have with Hillary. I knew the crippling facade between us had gone on for too long, yet here I am, still unable to come up with a way to bring it all to an end. Henry derives great pleasure in laughing at me whenever I bring up my situation with Hillary.

My eye catches a brown-skinned woman of an average height in a white tee, skinny black jeans, and high-top Converse. Her wild, curly hair is all over her face. As she shuffled through the airport. The load of her small car-ryon bag seemed to weigh her down as it dragged along behind her. She kept her head bowed and her eyes cast downward, like a fighter who had given up hope in the fight. It was almost as if her soul had already left the terminal, and only her body remained. Her beauty still shows despite her dejected demeanor.

She's the kind of beauty that stops you in your tracks. I notice a few guys checking her out, but she's oblivious to the attention. I keep my gaze on her, causing her to look my way. Our eyes locked, we held each other's eyes for a moment; she turns away, not even a smile or chuckle or a smirk escapes her. She just looks away. Like I'm irrelevant.

I felt a strange pull towards her, though she didn't seem like my usual type. On the one hand, I found her beauty captivating. On the other hand, I felt like nothing about her should have attracted me. It's just my body defying reason; because nothing about this woman fit my type, yet she inexplicably attracting me.

I shake off thoughts of her and turn my attention to my iPad, planning my work week. Hopefully, I can get this work done in three to five days and not be in Chicago for two weeks. Once the first-class boarding was called, I boarded right away. Surprisingly, the girl with the wild curls walks in and sits in the seat right beside me. Before I could say a word to her, my phone rings, and it's Hillary again. What could she possibly want right now?

"Hey, I can't talk right now, we just boarded," I say.

"Ok, I just wanted to know what you plan to wear to the wedding so I can coordinate my outfit with yours."

"Can I get back to you on that?"

"Sure, have a safe trip, honey."

"Thanks."

I hung up and switched my phone off. I noticed the lady beside me frantically rummaging through her purse. I wonder what she is searching for. I try to ignore her, though I notice her shaking hand and heavy breathing, beads of sweat on her forehead. She tries to control her breathing by inhaling and exhaling. Something is wrong.

Just as we are about to take off, her nervousness is obvious. Her grip is tight on the armrests, her controlled breathing isn't calming her. She probably has a fear of flying. I turned to her. "Are you alright?" I ask quietly.

"No, I have a fear of flying."

I watch as her anxiety builds. She's panting as she tries to steady her shaking hands.

"I always take a pill, and I just realized the pill is in the bag I checked. This day couldn't get any worse for me," she says.

"How can I help you?"

"Would you mind if I hold your hand as we take off?"

"I don't mind if it would help you."

She exhales. "Thank you," she says as I reach for her hand. When she turns to me, I'm mesmerized by her honey-colored eyes.

"Close your eyes and try to concentrate on my firm grip. I got you." She places her hand in mine. So soft, a jolt of electricity flows through me, my eyes widening in surprise. Her closed eyes fly open. We gaze at each other as the rumbling sound of the plane roars. She squeezes my hand tight and pants in fear. I hold on firmly to her.

"Keep taking deep breaths and focus on me." She nods.

Once in the air, her breathing slows. She loosens her grip on my hand and slowly let go of my hand. I immediately miss the absence of her touch. She then thanks me for my help and turns away, putting her earbuds in, but I want to talk with her.

As the flight progressed, she fell asleep. About an hour into the flight, the captain announced some minor issues, and our flight must divert to Colorado for the night.

Another chilly place. Again, why was I chosen one to visit Chicago? Aside from this beauty next to me, the entire trip is already feeling messed up.

We got off the plane and received our hotel passes for the night.

Once I checked into the hotel for the night, I noticed the same lady from the plane as I walked into the bar. I decided to speak to her.

"Hi," I say as she turns to me.

"Hi, thanks again for your help on the plane." She smiles widely and seems more relaxed. Happy even.

What a beautiful smile. I stand there admiring her caramel skin glowing under the light, her bright smile warming me up. "Mind if I join you?"

"Not at all. Please do." She stretched her hand to me. "I am Anne."

I shake her hand, realizing how much I like touching her.

"Philip," I reply.

"Nice to meet you and really, thanks again for being my support on the take-off." She smiles again.

"Any time." I place my order, and we talk about simple stuff. She tells me about her work as an interior decorator, and how she had moved to LA from Chicago after an endless job search. As we talk, she tells me how today had started terribly, then catching her boyfriend in amateur live porn, as she calls it, was the last straw to the dysfunctional day.

I quietly listen as she talks. I wonder if this is how Hillary feels about my cheating. Honestly, I wish she would break things off with me. Like Anne here says, she happily did.

As I listened to her, I thought to myself how much of an idiot her ex-boyfriend was, and I wanted to thank him for messing up. Otherwise, I wouldn't have met her. It occurred to me again how much I needed to break up with Hillary and not wait for her to get the message. I feel nothing but mutual respect for the woman. Not love, just two consenting adults. I couldn't care less if I didn't have any intimacy with her for months. Thinking about it, I haven't touched Hillary in months, and I haven't been starved either.

Anne smiling before me; however, I have a massive desire to touch, smell and taste.

The more she talked, the more I listened, and the more I liked her watching her talk and smile. Her round face with captivating honey-colored eyes light up as she speaks, when she smiles those full lips are certainly inviting. I want to touch her hair, something I've never cared to do before, but on Anne, I desire to touch and inhale everything about it.

As she talked, she tells me she flies the same airline at least once every month to Chicago. Anne was willing to tell me everything. Guess her shitty day or boyfriend breakup is making her open. She doesn't strike me as a woman that would normally talk this much. I don't mind and I'm just happy to keep her talking. She showed me pictures of her interior decoration collection and talked about how much she enjoyed decorating. She expressed so much passion for her job; It's clear she loves what she did.

The subtle flirtation of Anne smacking her lips and our intermittent locked gaze with her smiles is building me for more with her. We finished our dinner and headed towards our hotel rooms. It surprised me to find out we were on the same floor, with rooms across from each other. Pleasantly convenient, and who am I to complain about such luck?

Once we got to our doors, she said goodnight and turned to open her door. The card wouldn't work. I had my door open. I pulled her to me in and kissed her. We kicked my door closed, undressing each other hungrily. I dug the condom out of my wallet, unable to avoid admiring her beautiful, toned body and with that smile. I'm done for.

We were both panting after our bodies had swirled in earth-shattering sex.

"We need to do that again, so I know I didn't imagine it," she says, chuckling.

"You didn't imagine it, and do you still have the energy?"

"I certainly have twice the energy if you are offering the same pleasurable scenario," she flirts.

"Why don't we find out if I can up my beat my own best record?"

I pull my pants from the floor to grab another condom from my wallet, only to find out I am out of condoms. I sigh.

"Something wrong?" She looks longingly at me.

"I am out of condoms." My shoulder shrugs in disappointment.

"That's no fun. Well, I'm clean, and I can't get pregnant anyway, "she eagerly stated.

"I am super clean, if you're sure you don't mind and won't get pregnant."

"I am sure. Come here before the cautious me kicks in and I walk out."

"You don't have to ask me twice."

We spent the next few hours making fireworks over and over. I had fallen for her within a few hours. It can't be possible, but I'm willing to explore whatever this is.

"This is more than just sex; I am so sleepy, but can we talk in the morning, please..."

"Ok," she mutters tiredly.

The room wake-up call wakes me up. I turned, and she wasn't there. I thought maybe she went to her room to change, and we would meet downstairs. I thought of calling her, then realizing that I didn't have her number. That would be the first thing I get from her once we meet. I knocked on her door and got no response, so I headed for the lobby. While checking out, I asked about her, and I am told she checked out already. Why would she leave? What we shared was phenomenal; I hope she is not having second thoughts or feeling awkward, because I feel great.

As I looked around the terminal, I couldn't find her. Not having her full name makes it difficult to ask the attendant about her. I figured she would be on the flight anyway, so I stayed patient. When I boarded, it was a rude awakening when an older lady sat next to me. At first, I thought the lady had sat in the wrong seat and Anne would arrive soon to let her know, but as the plane fills with no Anne in sight, I had to ask the older woman.

"Did they change some seats from the prior flight?"

"I don't know. I wasn't on the prior flight. I need to be in Chicago urgently and the young lady that had this seat offered to exchange her ticket with me. She said her grandmother was stable and she could wait for the next flight."

"Thank you, Ma'am, enjoy your flight." I couldn't believe it. She was avoiding me so much that she traded her ticket. Well, I know where she works. I will find her. She can't change my life and walk away from what we shared.

I finished my task in Chicago, but not without spending every night playing back every second of my lovemaking with Anne. Each moment was so vivid in my mind, I could almost taste her and smell her.

I arrived back in LA after five days, still pining over Anne. When Hillary showed up, all the pining came to a complete halt, like a DJ suddenly changing a Rihanna song to a lullaby at the club. The 'It' factor I've now found, although I still refused to believe it. My mind creatively becomes calculative on how to break things off with Hillary amicably.

In fact, I figured I should get Hillary and all my unroyal wild oats out of the way before I went in search of Anne.

Six weeks after my return to LA, I concluded a plan on how Hillary and I would part ways and our families would remain friends. I tried to get my mind back to work and forget Anne. I couldn't take it anymore; my mind was going crazy about her meeting another man, so I went to her place of work. When I got there, I realized it was not a small company, and the fact Anne was the only name I had did not help. The next couple of weeks, I waited outside the building at random hours hoping to see her until I realized the building had four exits, hence why I didn't randomly find her.

It felt strange, almost like she'd never existed, but I know she was real. I guess it is true what they say. When something feels too good to be true, it probably is. That one night with her felt too good to be true.

Over the next two years, I had to convince myself that what I felt was not real, though it felt authentic.

I subconsciously put Anne on the backburner. I slowly let go of Anne and did what I swore I wouldn't do, which was get engaged to Hillary. I'd decided that since I cannot find and have Anne, I might as well stick with Hillary. But I wasn't in a rush to fully tie the knot with Hillary, so I continued to use every delay tactic to keep us from following through with the marriage. I continue to hold on to a sliver of hope that Anne might pop back into my life again, just as she had the very first time.

Three

CIARA

My night with Philip was amazing and mind-blowing, just as I couldn't believe I had slept with a stranger. I guess yesterday was so bad that I needed to find myself, but I do like Philip a lot. That wasn't just crazy amazing sex; there was more. I had multiple orgasms, something I never had with Kevin.

The sound of a phone vibrating had woken me up. I untangled myself from Philip, who was wrapped around me like a baby swaddle, and reached for the phone. It showed Hillary on the caller ID. At first, I wondered why she would call, but still a little sleepy, I answered it anyway.

"Hello?"

The voice yelled "HELLO" back.

"Hey Hill, relax," I said groggily.

"Are you the bitch he's sleeping with this week?"

My eyes flew wide open right away. Those words stung like a bitch slap over the phone.

"Excuse Me?" I ask quietly.

"Yeah, I know you are in bed with my boyfriend Philip, and you even dare to answer his phone. He usually keeps you trashy hook-ups on a leash, but since you decide to be bold, I will only say this once, get away from Philip before I find you. I won't be so nice when I do." she yelled.

"Now, put my fiancé on the phone and make sure you disappear," she commanded. I was in shock, my heart in turmoil. I just hung up, climbed out of bed, picked up my clothes, dressed quietly, and left the room. I went to my room to freshen up,, but I was a mess. I couldn't control the tears that wouldn't stop flowing. I pulled myself together and checked out of the hotel.

By the time I got to the gate, my inside was tearing up with memories of last night. Who was I fooling? It was just a night with a cute guy. What made me think it was going to be more than that? I had just broken up with a guy I'd dated on and off for four years, and I jumped in bed with a random cheating guy. I must have loser stamped on my forehead in neon.

Granted, Philip's hands on my body felt great, and that kiss had me reeling in seventh heaven. The unwritten agreement was for one night, and the time has come to walk away.

I was unsure of how I was going to face him once we got on the plane. I guess the best way to respond if he tries to talk to me is by saying, "It was one night, and today is a new day. Nothing gained, nothing lost." That sounded perfect to me, but it shattered my heart at the same time. I doubt he would respond to me once I say that, and I would have a great flight to Chicago, though, I subconsciously wish he would say I was wrong, but do I want another cheater?

As I sat at the gate watching people on the move, my subconscious practiced how to part ways with no gains or losses. I overhear a woman frantically asking if she could find a seat on my flight.

"Please, I really need to be in Chicago. It's an emergency. My son was in a car accident. Please see if there is an empty seat. I have a ticket for the next flight. That is another three hours. Wait, please check again," she says hysterically.

I watch as the attendee searches, and says, "Sorry ma'am, the flight is fully booked," as the lady let out a grunt before dialing on her phone to someone. The attendee asked if anyone will give up their seat.

My subconscious says to me, "This might save you an embarrassing moment, let the woman have your ticket, and you never have to see Philip again." I immediately got up once the thought was clear to me and walked up to the counter. The woman was so excited that she hugged me.

"Thank you so much," she said.

I tried not to fidget as the attendee took her time making the exchange. I want it to be done before he arrives, which I am sure will be soon. I had arrived super early after the nasty phone call. Once the exchange was done, I briskly moved to a close-by restaurant and took a seat furthest away from the gate.

He soon arrived, and I watched him from where I was seated. He is so fucking gorgeous, an epitome of tall, chiseled and handsome. Dark hair, brown sexy eyes, at least six feet tall with well-chiseled face and body. The man had muscles in the right places. I watch as he runs his hands through his hair, as he looks around for me. I lost count of how many times I did that, and he obviously can't see me in my vantage point, which is perfect.

I'm saving us both from a possible awkward moment. I bet his fiancée called him back after I hung up on her if she is that feisty over the phone. I do not want to imagine being in her presence. I feel a tear drop, and I immediately wipe it off. Just how am I crying over Philip, when less than twenty-four hours ago I walked out on a four-year relationship and didn't shed a tear? I watched him board the flight and more tears fell. A part of me genuinely felt loved being in his arms.

I sat there till they closed the gate and realized a part of me was gone on that flight. Face reality, I tell myself.

I arrived home hours later. Once I dropped my bags, I went straight to the hospital. By the time I got back home from visiting my grandmother, I felt a little better to be back home with my family. I spent the next eight days having fun with my sister and family and visiting my grandmother as many times as I could. Each time I am alone, my mind and body are on Philip, feeling every moment we touched, laughed, and made love. It felt too good to be true. As the end of my vacation approached, it was sad having to leave again and go across the country to be alone now that I no longer had a boyfriend.

I returned to LA a day before my vacation was over to get my stuff out of Kevin's apartment. At least he's no longer begging and asking; we make it work. We parted amicably, and I couldn't be happier. I stayed home alone before returning to work.

Back at work, I buried my head in every task; without my ex and no Philip, all I could do is work and hang out a few times with my girls Amy and Claire. Four weeks after I got back to work, always tired became the new me. I fall asleep at the drop of a hat. I would get to work super late; for me, tardiness was unacceptable. I also developed an appetite like no tomorrow with a craving for weird food, things I wouldn't normally want.

By the end of the seventh week, Amy encouraged me to see a doctor because sleeping during our conversation was not acceptable.

So, I made an appointment with her recommended doctor, who ordered a few blood tests, and eventually informed me I was about seven to nine weeks pregnant. I realized I had gained weight, but I thought it was because I was eating more, sleeping more, and exercising less. At first, I laughed and said she was joking because I'd been told I could not get pregnant, but it shocked me when the ultrasound picked up the heartbeat.

I sat there; the news numbing me; I could not for the life of me comprehend what was happening. I had tried for the last two years with Kevin to get pregnant, hoping it would somehow salvage our dying relationship. Because of my irregular period, sometimes heavy or sometimes light, or zero periods in some months, along with travel and Kevin never being in the mood, I had lost all hope of ever getting pregnant. Now, here I am, pregnant with the baby of a man I slept with once and fell head over heels for.

The shock of being told that I'm pregnant with Philip's baby was beyond me. Who do I talk to? How will I raise this child? My mind is in turmoil as I drove home alone with happy yet complex news. I called my sister and spoke with her; I didn't tell her about the pregnancy.

I spent the next few days in a world of my own, just pacing around my house. I will finally have the baby that I have always wanted; the only problem is there is no one to share it with. Amy asked several times about the doctor, and I lied saying I have another follow up appointment.

A month later, I went back for my next check, and they compounded my shock when they detected two heart-beats. How the hell did they miss this before? Not only am I pregnant, but I'm now having twins? Un-fucking believable. Philip's super sperm sure knows how to seal the deal. My life has changed completely. I'm confused about where to begin. I thought about going to Phillip, but how do I tell a one-night stand that I am pregnant with his baby—oh sorry babies, plural?

I'd done a good job of hiding my pregnancy. Amy called for lunch; she'd been asking me for the last few weeks what's going on with me. Once seated, Amy is never one to waste time with pleasantries.

"Are you going to tell me what the heck is going on with you?" she asks outright.

"I am pregnant with twins," I say with the restaurant menu up in my face. When I lower the menu and peep at her, her face is frozen. Then it changes to word pro-cessing, then unbridled excitement.

"Congratulations!" she yells.

"Shhhh," I respond.

"Come on, we are not underage girls, so this is great news. I am so happy for you." Excitement was all over her face. "Wait, you and Kevin broke up. How are you going to handle this?" Up until this moment, I hadn't mentioned my night with Phillip to anyone. It had been my secret. I was reluctant to reveal anything. It occurred to me I could share just the amount I want her to know, not all of it.

"It's not Kevin's," I answer.

"What! You have been seeing someone and didn't tell me?" Of course, only in Amy's world is it bad for me to keep anything private.

"No, I'm not seeing anyone. I had a one-nightstand on my flight to Chicago a few months ago."

"What! A mile-high club knocked you up?" she exclaims in excitement.

"Amy, can you be any louder? I don't think the other guests heard you," I remarked, then took a deep breath and continued. "Our flight had to divert because of a mechanical issue. They set us up in a hotel for the night, and we had dinner together and ended up in bed together; that's all," I stated, hoping that was enough.

"You will not hold out on me; I want full disclosure." She firmly states with that expression of don't mess with me.

"There isn't much to tell. I had just caught Kevin with his head in between another woman's legs, so we broke up. I was a little emotional after that, and the guy I met was nice, good looking, well chiseled and seemly available. I have always been proper, so I thought why not," I say calmly, although my mind sometimes whirls at how irresponsible my action was.

"Yeah, girl, why not!?" Omg! Amy is loving this too much.

"My 'why not' has led to twins. Why can't I do something like that without someone finding out? Why did my shit and inappropriate behavior have to come out and not stay hidden?"

"Come on now, don't beat yourself up. If it wasn't meant to be, it wouldn't have happened considering you have been trying to get pregnant with miserable Kevin. A one-night stand with this guy turned into twins, so I say it is a good thing."

"The real question, Ciara Anne Kellington, is are you going to find him and tell him, or do you plan to do this alone?" I never like it when she uses my full name and gives me a stern look.

"I think I might do this alone; I don't know where to find him," I lie.

"You don't sound like you want to try and find him."

"I don't, because he's engaged, and I don't want my babies or our one night to ruin whatever happily never after they have. I will raise my babies alone. To be honest, I'm not sure how I am going to manage, but I will figure it out."

"Well, you know Claire and I have always had your back."

"Thanks, I know you guys do."

"Ciara, do you at least have his name?"

"No," I lie again. Of course, I have his name. At the hotel checkout, the lady had checked me out of the wrong room and gave me papers with his name on it. I then called her attention to the error. Philip Webster is a name I would never forget, but I don't want to share any more details about him. I just might carry these details to my grave.

"Well, look at it this way. You always wanted a baby, now you have two, so I say congratulations, and you know I will always be perfect aunty Amy."

"Thanks Amy, I know." We changed the topic to work and all the fun in Amy's life.

As my days turned into weeks, my body could barely hold me. I became sick and ended up on restricted bed rest for a few weeks. I did not tell my family since they were all worried about my grandma, plus I didn't know how to explain my pregnancy to them. I made excuses each time it was my regular schedule to fly home. I convinced Steven, my best friend, not to come and visit me yet.

Amy and Claire came over and spent the night with me a few times to help me, which was great because I needed the help. I couldn't eat without throwing up my guts.

As I started to feel better, my boss allowed me to work from home whenever possible, which was great.

Five months into my pregnancy, it's Amy's birthday, and she decided to celebrate at a fancy restaurant. I'm feeling better and able to get out more. I was thrilled to have found a parking spot right in front of the restaurant, which was shocking. I was maneuvering my car into the spot when I see Phillip walking into the restaurant with a woman; their arms were wrapped around each other. She was all smiles and giggles. My shaking hands were eager to punch and break her pretty face with screams in her face saying I am pregnant and fat with his children, and I don't know what my body feels like anymore. I am always in the bathroom. Do you really want to say that? My subconscious invades. I release my tight grip on the steering wheel and watch them walk in. They are seated in a spot that would make it easy for him to see me if he's able to unwrap himself from the woman.

I can't take the chance of him seeing me; he could turn away and act like he doesn't know me, or he could walk up to me. If he did that, I could almost see myself exploding in his face, which leaves me with a third option of completely avoiding a possible encounter and just head home. I went with the third option, so I texted Amy apologizing, saying that I wasn't feeling good, and I couldn't make it.

I drove back, not too happy with myself, but I couldn't take the chance of him seeing me pregnant and asking questions. I doubt he would think it was his, and I also doubt I could control my hormones from yelling, "the babies are yours" in his face.

Amy and Claire, being exceptional friends, stopped over at my place that night, and guilt ate at me because I couldn't tell Amy the truth. We spent the night in my apartment having our mini party.

Four weeks later, my sister called me to tell me my grandmother had passed. I cried so much as I packed my bags for Chicago. I was so caught up in mourning my grandmother that I completely forgot that I had told no one in my family about my pregnancy.

My family nearly passed out when they saw my belly. They couldn't believe I had not told them about my pregnancy. My drained and overwhelming reaction to Grandma's death made it impossible for them to question me; they just accepted me.

After the funeral, a surprise revelation was finding out my grandma had left my sister and me $250,000 each. She left her house to my parents. I could not believe the old bird had that much money saved up. I can now afford to quit my job in LA and move back to Chicago, I thought to myself when the will was read. Being with my family again made me realize that staying in LA alone was not worth the trouble, the pain, and the possibility of running into Phillip.

Once I returned to LA, I started my plans to move back to Chicago. I could raise my children close to my family and would have more hands-on-deck to help with the babies. The reality of not raising my children alone sounded better when I thought about moving back home.

Amy wasn't happy about my move, but she understood; she has always had my back. Most of my friends have been great, too, but she was right there at the top.

My family and friends welcomed me back with open arms. I bought a house, a new car, and used some of the money to start my design company. It was like a dream come true. My genteel Iranian grandmother was my fairy godmother in a twisted way. Her sickness led me to meet Philip, where I got gifted with my magical twins, and her financial gift gave me the opportunity to start my business and be close to family.

By my third trimester, as my babies grew, my movement became slower, but I had the babies' room set up. I know now that I am having fraternal twins: a boy and a girl. We set their room up in neutral colors.

My sister brought up the subject of the twins' father, and I told her I did not want to talk about it. She realized right away that I had not told him and warned me it might not be a comfortable experience if he found out about his children.

She tried to get more information about him, but all I said was that his name is Philip, and I don't want to talk about it, and that's the end of the discussion.

My best friend Steven, which everyone still finds strange that we are besties, asked more about Philip and I told him everything. I guess I can leave the secret about my babies' father in his hands and not carry it to my grave.

The next few weeks went by as I struggled about whether I should find Philip and tell him about the babies. My family tried yet again to find out who the father was, but I utterly refused to tell them. I'd, of course, found out more about Philip and discovered how rich he is.

I concluded it's best I let sleeping dogs lie. Why go to him with news of a wild one-night turned into magical twins? He probably forgot all about me, considering I told him I couldn't get pregnant, plus his girlfriend pretty much said I was the girl of the week.

Seven and a half months into my pregnancy, I woke up with lots of pain. Thankfully, my mom had spent the night at my place and drove me to the hospital. By the time we arrived, I was in severe pain; both babies had to be delivered immediately. Filipa and Finn were born premature. Filipa gained weight with time, but Finn was not getting better. The doctors did all they could, but he eventually died a little over a week after birth.

I thought nothing could rip my heart out until Finn died. I fell into my mother's arms and wept uncontrollably. My family surrounded me with love, but I couldn't get up and take care of my daughter, so my mom and sister took care of her for a few days. That was the moment in life when I truly understood the power of having your family close.

A couple of days later, my mom gently told me I had to get out of bed and that my daughter needs me as well. I

had to be strong for her. She brought her to me and laid
her right next to me. As I watched her sleep, I realized
that my mother was right. Finn was gone forever, and it
was just the two of us against the world.

I carried her and held her in my arms, and I slowly began
to smile. My mom peeped in on us, and I smiled at her
saying, "Thank you, mom." My life soon revolved around
my daughter, work, and family. Business was growing at
a perfect pace.

As Filipa turned one, my conscience pricked me: Philip
still does not know about his daughter.

My annoying best friend had brought up the issue again
as I continued to think about whether or not to call him.

The final decision not to tell Philip and keep my baby
to myself happened when my sister brought home a
magazine showing Philip is engaged. The headline read,
"**It's Finally Official: Philip Webster and Hillary Sloan
Getting Married.**" the paper went into details about the
romantic way he proposed and the whole affair with
them.

They apparently had been dating for over five years.
His family already considered Hillary part of their family.
Philip's parents were said to be delighted, especially his
mother. The union of Philip and Hillary is viewed as a
powerhouse in his social circles.

As I read the details, I wiped away my tears, realizing
Philip and I never even had a chance. This led me to

finalize my decision that Filipa was all mine, and Philip would never find out about her.

He can start his life with Hillary and be happy.

My life as a single mother continued pleasantly with my daughter.

Steven got engaged to Vivienne, his beautiful Italian girl-friend; I love everything about her except the fact that she talks too damn much. There were times I wanted to tape her mouth shut to keep her quiet.

Steven can always sense whenever her spill is killing me. He always gives me a look that said, 'please stay calm and don't blow up in her face'. As time went by, Steven and I worked on a few projects together. He also brought his buddy James to join his business.

James, Steven, and I went to high school together. I hadn't seen James in years. Steven told me he recently broke his engagement and moved back to Chicago from Texas. James is just as tall as Steven; standing together, I can't tell who's taller. My best friend is a dark-haired, blue-eyed white boy, as I like to call him, and James is biracial like me. Both handsome looking guys, which is why I get the nasty look from ladies whenever I am out with them.

Steven and James have formed a partnership in the construction business; each brings a unique skill that complements the other. I am the ultimate piece to the puzzle with my designs.

James is a pretty laid-back guy, amiable and always willing to help. Not sure if the help part was just for me, but I could tell my daughter loved playing with him.

Eventually, James and I started dating casually. I'm not looking for a father for my daughter, and I don't have any special feelings for James, although my sister advised me to give him a chance, and said that in time, I would come to love and appreciate him.

We continued dating and continued our work together. My daughter just continued to be a happy child. She was no doubt Philip's daughter because of her looks. I don't see me in her except for when she shows her stubborn side, which makes me dread the teenage years ahead.

About eighteen months after Filipa was born, my friend Claire would not take no for an answer about my coming to LA for her wedding. She even asked me to bring James, since I had mentioned him a few times, and sent me an invite for two. I didn't think I was ready to introduce James and I as a couple, so I didn't mention the invite to James. I was going to go alone and have fun with my friends.

Amy was super excited that I was going to the wedding; she had visited me a few months after Filipa was born. She also wanted to meet James, but I told her I was not feeling any attraction towards James. I've even avoided having sex with him since we started dating. Though I admit, he's a great guy and would be perfect if I was thinking marriage, but I do not have marriage on my radar. Unfortunately, my sister keeps nudging me towards him.

Four

CIARA

This is my first time away from my daughter since she was born and I'm having anxiety about leaving her. My sister, Stella, and my parents were traveling out of town, so I saw that as an excuse to cancel my going to the wedding.

However, Steven and Vivienne wouldn't allow me to bail; they offered to take Filipa for the weekend. I bet I drove them bonkers, asking them over and over if, they were sure.

I ended up going to LA for the wedding and relaxed a ton after a few glasses of alcohol in me with Amy by my side cheering me on.

I FaceTime with Filipa before the wedding who was being spoiled and did not mind that I was away.

Amy had checked us into the hotel, which I quickly realized was one of the Webster family chains. Claire, the Bridezilla, had booked all her wedding activities here. At first, I wanted to change hotels, but I couldn't find a valid excuse. Of course, the booked hotel is high end, and we were going to have the time of our lives, so I had to convince myself that there was no way Philip would be at this hotel. Just because his family owned it doesn't mean he lives here or would be there.

Silly, enjoy yourself and check out first thing on Sunday evening without worries. He's probably busy with his bride to be, I tell myself.

The bachelorette party and all the wild wedding activities were in full swing. Something I didn't realize I'd missed in the last few years. Amy dragged me out during the wedding reception for a quiet moment to talk. We were seated having our moment as she told me about the stunt her boyfriend had pulled. I could not help myself; I laughed out loud, not caring about my surroundings. We were having a girlish moment when she suddenly stopped laughing and looked somewhere else.

Standing before me is Philip. The one man I was sure I wouldn't see in this hotel this weekend. How the hell did this happen and why did he come closer to me and not walk away like he didn't know me? I avoid his eyes as I dust imaginary lint off my sage bridesmaid dress. I tuck my hair behind my ear a few times. Amy is giving me the weird Amy look where her eyebrow is raised, and her eyes dig into mine. I can also feel Philip's gaze roving over me and I'm more self-conscious to his look than Amy's weird eyes.

I decided to be a big girl and talk to him. "Hi Philip," I smile. He doesn't respond as we stare at each other until Amy cleared her throat. I introduced him to Amy, who realized right away that she'd be a crowd in this conversation and excused herself. Philip immediately took the seat vacated by Amy.

I can't believe he's right here in front of me, almost three years, and he looks like he hasn't aged a day. I ache to touch him. I'm still very attracted to him nearly three years later, and nothing has changed. All I could do is try to hide the force that keeps drawing me to him; hopefully I am doing a good job, though I sense I am failing woefully.

He continues to smile at me, and I need him to stop looking at me with such blatant desire, like he's doing right now, to break the ice, I say,

"Congratulations on your engagement! When is the official date?" Is it my imagination, or did the smile just fade? He didn't answer my question; instead, he changed the subject. We talked like the very first time we'd met. He insisted on being my plus one at Claire's wedding. I couldn't have asked for a better plus one. However, that secret stays with me.

I introduced Philip to my friends at our table. Amy gave me a look that signaled, nice catch, and welcomed Philip like we had always hung out like this. Lots of laughter. He wouldn't let go of me, and I was just as happy to hold on to him all night. When we danced and he pulled me close, his fresh scent filled my nostrils. Laughter was the best way to hide the enthralling scents of him.

After the bride and groom left, we sat down talking. I talked about my new designs and work mostly, making sure not to mention the fact that I had moved to Chicago and certainly not about Filipa. Nothing about the children. As we talk, I can tell he assumes I am still living in LA; I say nothing to change his assumptions. I simply went along with it. Not sure if it's a good plan, but I'm not about to tell him now that we have a daughter. For all I know, this may be just another night and nothing more. After all, he's very much engaged, and I have not had sex since the last time I slept with him. Until now, sex had become dormant in my body; not getting it and not missing it.

Though James and I aren't "officially" dating. Our relationship is still in that early stage, where all we do is hug and share a few kisses. James has undoubtedly tried to increase our sexual activity, but I have found it challenging to go beyond a few kisses with him. Almost like I could not share my body with any other man since Philip.

James, I must confess, has been sweet about giving me time. They all think I'm mentally affected because I don't know who Filipa's father is. I have refused to share his full name with them. My sister thinks I refused to disclose who my baby daddy is because I had an affair with a married man, or I had a drunk one-night stand

and can't remember who I slept with. If only she knew my memory of that night is very vivid.

The presence of Philip next to me right now is almost unbearable, his piercing brown eyes locked in a gaze with mine.

Every subtle touch is triggering alarms all over my body. I'm trying hard to hold it together and he's not helping with his open stares and subtle touch. As we danced, he wrapped those perfectly toned arms around my waist and pulled my body to a perfect mold with his. He breathily whispers in my ears, sending flames of desire through my body, awakening every sexual cell. My nipples are awake and begging to be kissed and panties are wet, which isn't good in a silky dress.

When the music stopped, it took a minute for us to realize we were alone on the dance floor. Our hands interlaced when we return to our seat with Amy's eyes shouting what the fuck!

I downed my glass of wine to calm my tightly strung nerves and possibly quench the waves of desires. He tells me about two women; I could not believe two different women tried to pass their children off as his. I teased him a little about it.

"What did Hillary think of these women?" I ask.

"She assumed they were all gold diggers, since I was certain I wasn't the father of either woman's child."

"How could you have been so sure?"

"Well, I only slept with one, and I used protection, which I was certain did not tear, and I have never slept with the other. She was just a psycho. I'll tell you a secret, actually two secrets."

"Whoa, two secrets? Lucky me." I smiled, rolling my eyes.

"One, you're the only woman I have had sex with within the last five years without a condom, and two, just to make their disturbing noise disappear, I almost agreed to give them money, but my father said no. Wise man." He smirks.

"He said if I give them money, then more women would seek to continue to milk me."

"A sagacious man," I acquiesce.

"What did you do then?"

"Power of science called DNA testing, and just like I had said, neither child was mine."

"Just curious. What would you have done if one of them was truly yours?" I calmly ask, maintaining a jaunty expression.

"Tough question, only because I would hate to be tied to either woman forever, but I would have fought for full custody."

"Really? Why and how would you have done that?"

"First, I know one woman was on drugs, and I would not let any child of mine be raised around drugs. Second, I doubt either of them is fit to be a mother. To them, a child is a means to an end."

"Just those two reasons, not because it is your child, and you love that child?"

"Would have loved the child if it was mine, but it was not, so I am a free man," he says, smiling.

My heart is in turmoil as I listen to him, I guess it is a good thing that I have not mentioned Filipa, he might see me as a gold digger as well and want full custody out of a crazy sense of loyalty, not love. It's impossible for me to see his fiancée taking care of any child; she is a real socialite.

"So, tell me about your fiancée," I said.

"No, I will not talk about her when I am with you," he replies sternly. "Are you seeing anyone?" he asks instead.

"No," I reply knowing damn well that I was lying.

Our conversation continued to cover topics we briefly discussed the last time we were together. Until the cleaning crew informed us they had to lock up.

We walked to the elevator, and I thought he was just going to walk me to the elevator and say goodnight. I was surprised when he stepped in and pressed the button for the penthouse.

I know I should say something, but I want him so badly. I've not had sex in over three years. Since he walked up to me in the hotel lobby, and during every moment he's touched me, I have craved him.

The moment we walk into his room, our clothes started flying. We are all over each other as if our souls needed to merge instantly.

Philip makes love to me like he had the secret key to unlocking every hidden part of my body, which also awakens him once he unlocks it.

Loud moans of pleasure accompanied every toe-curling moment. I curled up beside him like this is where I belong. I couldn't believe I'm lying in his arms again. He is truly my sexual match!

He is engaged, you idiot, I remind myself. What am I doing sleeping with him again? A guy who continually cheats on his fiancée. I got up and went to my purse to check my phone and called Steven to check on my Filipa. The moment he answered, I knew something was wrong with his shaky tone.

"Ciara I am so sorry, Filipa fell and broke her arm, we are at the ER."

"What!" I shouted. "How the hell did that happen?"

"She was playing around, and I didn't see her coming when I bumped her into the wall hard, and she broke her left arm. I know you are worried, but the doctors said she would be ok."

My heart is pounding, my worst fear. I can't lose my daughter. "Please tell me the truth, Steven."

"Ciara, she's fine and sleeping." He sends a picture of her cast arm. I listened to him telling me everything the doctor said. Here I am having sex and my child is in pain and crying in the ER with a broken arm, all without her mother. I rush to put my clothes on.

"I am on my way home, Steven. I will see you in a few hours."

I'm leaving Philip again. I need to figure out how he would react to finding out about Filipa, so I don't bother waking him.

I wrote my phone number, full name with the message "family emergency, I had to leave, but please call me." Ciara Anne Kellington. 312-555-2505. We need to talk."

The four-hour flight felt like a lifetime. I miss Philip, but I was also worried about our daughter. My mind was all over the place.

Arriving in Chicago, Steven tells me they were home with Filipa. I found her eating a big bowl of ice cream and enjoying all the attention they were giving her. Though I was upset, I couldn't fight with Steven, and he looked sad.

Once I got Filipa in bed, my mind once again made me aware of how much I missed Philip. I sat on the edge of her bed; I realized how upset I would be if Steven had not told me about Filipa's injury. Realizing I would feel worse if I didn't even know she existed.

I will tell Philip about her once he calls me. For now, I will enjoy the moments with my daughter before I must share her with Philip.

Five weeks later

I'm back into my life like nothing significant happened in LA. Philip didn't call me back after our night. For the first couple of days, I regularly checked my phone. By the time days turned into weeks, I had concluded it was just a fling, like the first time.

Why I thought we had anything special was just plain stupid of me. I turned my focus to work and tried as much as possible to give more attention to James, whom I had finally accepted as my boyfriend. He loves Filipa, and she loves him back, which to me is just simply perfect.

Though work was fine, and my projects were good, I just couldn't stop thinking about Philip. Whenever I am alone, I constantly stare at the pictures of us that were taken by Amy, unbeknownst to us. She'd sent me the photos a week after the wedding. I had them stored on my phone and I would look at the pictures as if we were two people in love with no knowledge of each other.

James and I would go out together and sometimes have quiet moments in the house with Filipa. He would steal kisses, but I couldn't let him go beyond that. I could tell he wants more, but I can't go to bed with him. It would be a gross mistake since I am still pining for Philip. I let James know I am not ready to be intimate; he seemed willing to accept that for now.

After my return from LA, my family kept asking more about Filipa's father, but I still refused to disclose his identity.

Today, Filipa was pulling on James to take her to the park. I packed up their bags and said goodbye. Once inside, I placed an order for Jimmy John's. I had barely sat down when my bell rang. I headed to the door and made sure I had the exact change in hand. I opened it as I stretched my hand out with the money, hoping to receive a sandwich. Someone pulled my hand, opening the door wider. Before me stands Philip.

My legs gave away from the shock and no food all day. I opened my eyes to Phillip holding me. I can't believe he is here.

Five

PHILIP

Three years later, my hopes and dreams of finding Anne were unfulfilled. I sit in our large hotel bar enjoying a drink with Henry, who, as always, was so happy to remind me of my failed attempts at breaking up with Hillary. He emphasized my sad situation by pointing out to me that not only did I not break things with her, but I'm now officially engaged to her. I just sat there and took all the jabs, upset, but the truth is he's calling me out on my dumb moves. Sipping my drink, I hear the laughter and voice that had filled my dreams for the last few years. At first, I thought it was the universe playing tricks on me as I did a double take toward the sound.

Anne is sitting a few feet away from me and laughing hysterically at something a friend had said to her. I sat in my chair, transfixed, as I watched her laugh and smile. Henry tried to call my attention. I simply ignored him, placed my drink on the table, and walked towards the one woman that made my heart race.

I moved like a robot to where she was and stood there, staring at her. I couldn't believe I'd found her. She didn't see me at first, but it only took seconds for her to turn in my direction as she felt my intense stare.

"Hi," was all I could mouth once I was in front of her.

"Hi Philip," she responded without breaking my gaze.

"Am I imagining, or are you really here?" She chuckled at my words.

"Very nice to see you again, Philip."

My palm wipes my eyes, since it felt like an utter miracle that she was sitting in front of me. I wanted to pull her into my arms and kiss her senseless, but I had to play it cool. This beautiful woman had been haunting my dreams for almost three years.

"Great, I am certainly not imagining because you just said my name twice."

Her friend's throat clearing, and h-e-l-l-o drawl broke our gaze.

"Am sorry, Amy, this is an old friend of mine, Philip." I reached my hand out and shook Amy's.

She must have noticed our focus on each other, but she simply said, "Nice to meet you," and turned to Anne.

"I'll be waiting at our table, Ciara; see you soon," she said as she walked away.

"Ciara?" I asked, looking quizzically at her.

"Ciara is my first name, and Anne is my middle name."

"Well, that certainly explains a lot," I replied.

"So, nice to see you again. How have you been?" she asked, trying to have a casual conversation. As far as I am concerned, we were miles ahead of that. All I wanted to know was: Why did you leave my room, and why did you trade your ticket?

She puts her head down shyly while avoiding eye contact.

"I had never done anything like that before. Plus, I accidentally answered your phone, thinking it was mine. The name said Hillary flashed, and I thought it was my co-worker, but the lady on the other end cursed me out pretty good. I realized in less than 24 hours I was doing exactly what I broke up with Kevin about. I didn't want to cause you any more trouble with her, and I wasn't sure if you wanted to see me the next morning, so I left before you woke up. When I arrived at the gate and overheard a lady pleading to get a seat on the airplane for her to get home to her sick son. I traded my ticket with hers. I am sorry if that made you upset. You must understand; before that night, I had only been with my ex-boyfriend."

Just great, Hillary was the reason she left me. Three years only to find out Hillary was at the core. I do not even want to imagine what Hillary must have said to her, considering how it scared her off.

"That night was very new for me, and it was great," she continued, interrupting my thoughts.

"Me too," I blurted out... which made her smile. Oh, that bewitching smile of hers.

"I heard you are engaged. Congratulations on your engagement! When is the date?" she says.

Just as I wanted to shout at her and say, do not congratulate me. Instead, I said, "I went to your company to find you, of course, it was impossible since all I had was Anne, and they said no one by the name of Anne worked there."

She chuckled. "I am sorry, I gave you Anne because it felt like I was beginning a new chapter in my life, and I wanted to start it fresh, so I gave you my middle name, but everyone calls me Ciara."

"Would you prefer I call you Anne?"

"Ciara is fine."

"Can we go somewhere and talk? I have a lot to say to you."

She looked surprised. "I am here for one of my closest friend's wedding. I can't ditch now."

"Well, I am not about to let you disappear. I will have to crash the wedding."

She laughs.

"You seem so sure that I'm not here with a date."

"Well, are you?"

" No, I am not. My plus one could not make it, so you can be my plus one."

"Then it's settled."

I am not sure I want to know about her plus one. All I want is to be next to her. For three years I've waited for this moment, and I'm not going to let any of it pass me by. I turned my phone off. No interruptions with Ciara. God knows Hillary picks the craziest hour and minute to call me about the stupidest stuff.

We went to the wedding together and sat with her friends, who she introduced me to as an old friend. Sitting with her friends felt like this was our norm.

Like we had always shared jokes with friends and had a great time at a party. By the time the bride and groom said their goodbyes, Ciara and I talked, danced, and laughed till the late hours. Most of her friends had left, saying they would see her at a planned lunch the next day. I, of course, planned to be at the scheduled lunch with her. I would not let her out of my sight.

We were so engrossed in each other that the cleaning crew had to remind us they were closing. When they came around, we got up and walked towards the elevator. I didn't bother to ask her what her room number was. During our talk, I found out about the bridal party, and most guests were staying at the hotel, which put a smile on my face. That way, Ciara will not have to leave. I swiped my card for the penthouse and grabbed her as the elevator door closed.

I couldn't help being this close to her and not feel her in my arms. As soon as our lips touched, I knew how much I had been yearning for her. "I need to feel your naked body next to mine, no clothes between us. Nothing else, just us, completely naked and loving every moment," I mumbled into her ear.

We made it to the penthouse, and I grabbed her again. Her dress zipper came down fast, so did my shirt and pants. We made love to each other as though we had been starved of each other. I wanted to fill my hunger with every inch of her. By the time we lay next to each other, we were spent. I pulled her to me; I am a happy and satisfied man. Tomorrow is going to be a great day as I drift off to sleep.

I woke up and reached for Ciara, and to my surprise, she was not there. In a panic, I jumped out of bed and pulled my boxers on to look around. I checked the bathroom, and she was not there either. "Ciara?" I called out but got no answer. I realized her clothes were gone, too. No! This can't be happening again; why would she leave me again? I know without a doubt that we are great together. I heard movement in the living and raced towards the room; It shocked me to see Hillary holding a piece of paper in her hand.

"Who is she?" Hillary yelled at me.

"Give me the paper, Hillary," I requested, reaching my hand out to her. "Where is she?"

"Whoever she is, she left before I got here. How dare you sleep with another woman and throw it in my face!" she screams, obviously upset. But I couldn't care less about how angry she is.

"Give me the paper, Hillary," I repeated sternly.

"You show no remorse for sleeping with her. Ciara Anne Kellington or whoever the whore may be, left you her phone number and address stating she is sorry she had to leave for an emergency. I bet another sucker like you called. Imagine the audacity," she continues to express her disgust.

"Give me the paper, Hill," I repeated.

"I will do no such thing. You will never see her again. You and I are engaged, Phillip. I forgive you for this behavior, because I'll be damned if I let some whore take you from me. I have sacrificed too much for us," she said as she began ripping the paper.

"NO!" I exclaimed, racing to her. She runs towards the open window.

Before I could get to her, she threw the ripped paper out the window. I watched every contact of Ciara that I could have fluttered away in the wind. Anger filled me as I shoved Hillary onto the sofa.

"You and I are over," I yelled at her.

"We can't be over Philip Webster; we are engaged. What you had is a one-night stand, and if you think you can break up with me over some cheap lay, you are joking," she sneers.

"The engagement is off," I yelled at her, taking a deep breath to rein in my anger. "Off! Do you hear me? Now give me back my keys and get the hell out of my apartment before I do the unthinkable," I continued with the rage in me.

She began her fake sob. Something that has always worked on me before, but today it only fills me with rage.

"Hillary, give me my keys and get the fuck out now before or I throw you out myself," I shouted.

She picked up her bag, threw my keys on the floor, and walked out. I rushed to grab my phone and realized, not wanting to share the moment I had with Ciara; I had turned my phone off. My mind is raging. Another amazing night and she is gone. I turned my phone on and called Henry while ignoring the multiple outrageous messages from Hillary.

"Hey man, you just walked away with that girl and did not look back."

"That was Anne."

"You mean the same Anne from three years ago?"

"Yes."

"Wait, a minute; why did you say that was?"

"I lost her again."

"You are not making any sense."

"We spent the night together, and when I woke up, she was gone. She had left me her contact information, only I did not get to see the information because Hillary stopped by here and ripped it, then threw it out the window. All I have is a first name, middle name, and a vague idea of her last name."

"What is her name?"

"Ciara Anne."

"Nice name, but what did you do all that time yesterday that you didn't get all her information?"

"We talked about everything, and I figured she would wake up with me, not leave me a note."

"Something must have spooked her or called her attention. That's why she left you a note, so you have to wait till Monday to find her."

"Monday morning feels like forever, man."

"Do you want me to come over?"

"No, I will be fine; I broke up with Hillary."

"What!"

"You and I know I couldn't marry her, it was time I did, anyway. Right now, I feel like killing her."

"I feel you man, call me if you need me."

"I will, thanks, man."

I can't believe I have lost contact with Ciara again. Back in my bedroom, I stared at the bed, almost like I could see us there again. I smell her scent on my sheets. I spent the next few hours brooding around my house. Nothing appealed to me. All I want is Ciara back in my arms. I don't know where the wedding lunch party is being held on Sunday. The only information I have is that it is not in the hotel building. Just my luck when it comes to this woman.

My first place to look Monday morning is at her workplace. I don't have much to go by, but at least I have a first and middle name and a vague idea of her last name.

To my utter shock, when I arrived, I was told Ciara Anne quit about three years ago, and they had no forwarding information for her. The receptionist said she thinks she moved to Chicago, but she wasn't certain. Why would she not mention that to me? I then asked about her friend Amy, who I had met over the weekend. The receptionist said Amy was on vacation and due back in two weeks. I couldn't come up with any other name. Ciara had mentioned Amy as her only work friend, and I didn't have any information about the other friends.

My selfishness in wanting her to myself had blinded me to the fact that I needed to get all her information first. Now I could not reach her. I have to wait two weeks for Amy to return my only link to Ciara.

I sat in my car, not knowing what to do. I am filled with anger because of Ciara leaving and Hillary ripping up my only means of contact.

As I sat in my car, I played back every word of our conversations in my head; I can't believe she did not tell me she changed jobs. I told her everything, even the women that had claimed to be pregnant for me. How I had proposed to Hillary, though I did not feel I would ever truly marry her. Why would she not tell me where she works now or moved to?

I returned to work to face my mom, brooding about my breakup with Hillary. I watched her yap away about how humiliating it must be for Hillary and how I had to call Hillary and beg her to take me back and tell her I was confused. I just let her rant on until she said, "And that whore you were with, you need to forget her and make sure she doesn't come after you for money."

"Mom, I love you, and you can rant all you want about Hillary and me, but one thing I want you to cease from ever calling Ciara is a whore. I don't know what Hillary told you, but she and I are permanently over," I calmly informed her.

"Philip Carter Webster, you will not speak to your mother like that. I have told Hillary to give you time to come to your senses and realize you are making the worst mistake of your life."

"Just great, if you don't mind, I have a lot of work to do."

"You are kicking me out?"

"No, I actually have a conference call right now unless you wish to remain quiet for a potential hour-long call about land and buildings." I bet that got to her, she picked up her bag and walked out.

I tried everything to find Ciara Anne, but nothing happened. I hired a private investigator to search for Ciara Anne Kellington in LA. I gave the name of last company she worked for in LA . If no luck, search in Chicago. Didn't help that I didn't have a picture. I had to describe her to him. I also took the new expansion project Henry was working on in Chicago. I surprised him by taking the project, but to find Ciara I needed to cast a wide net of possibilities. Now I fly to Chicago on the same commercial airline we met since she mentioned she uses the same airline for points.

Four weeks later, while I was waiting for my flight at the airport, I overheard two ladies talking. I was seated just a seat away from the two ladies, so I heard their conversation even though I normally don't care about other people's conversations. Free entertainment, I guess.

"Oh, I have a better story," said the brunette lady to the African American sitting next to her. The African American had been chatting away about a friend's love story.

I could have taken the private jet, but I put myself through this torture for the chance. I might run into Ciara again.

"Can your story be better than mine?" asked the black woman.

"Here it goes. My fiancé's best friend is a woman. Just thought I mention that."

"Really, Steven's best friend is a woman?"

"Yes, she is amazing, though boyish, in my opinion."

I want to hear this story too, I thought to myself. Could save me the boredom of sitting here alone.

"Anyway, she was having the worst day of her life when she met the most amazing man, as she calls him the love of her life."

"You don't say, do tell."

"Yes, do tell," I murmured under my breath.

She goes into the full story of a lady having a bad day as I listened. I realized the story sounded too familiar and very personal to me. Now my ears are up.

"So, what happened afterward?" the black lady asked.

Please keep quiet. My life is about to change, I thought.

"Wait, here is the best part. Two months later, she finds out she is pregnant; her world was shattering because she was told she couldn't get pregnant, and here she was, pregnant. She was happy but couldn't share with the guy."

"Oh my God, she can't find him," the black lady said.

"No, she can. Turns out he's a rich and popular guy."

"So why doesn't she tell him?"

"Well, things happened. She found out she was pregnant with twins, and her grandmother died about six-plus months into the pregnancy and left her a nice chunk of money; she bought a house and moved back to Chicago permanently and started a small business."

"Whoa! She is a single mother of twins; why didn't she call him?"

"She was going to call him when she saw the engagement announcement of the guy with another woman. She thought there was no reason to ruin the union with information about her pregnancy, so she kept quiet. By the way, my fiancé let the little information about him and the fact he's engaged slip. He made me swear not to tell anyone and not to let her know I know the full story, so please keep this to yourself. Her family doesn't know." She continues, "Unfortunately, when she had the babies, one died a week after."

"Oh my God!" said the black lady. "And she still didn't call him?"

"No, she figured, why call him with the information? He is starting a new life with another woman and probably would not want her baggage, so she didn't."

"She started dating another guy, though. Well, a few weeks ago, a friend from LA called her and insisted she had to come to her wedding. She tried to get out of the wedding, but the friend would not have it any other way so, off to LA she went, for the wedding."

"Now, here is where it gets interesting; she runs into the same guy again at the wedding."

"Oh my, what happened?"

The brunette chuckles. "It keeps getting interesting. She ended up sleeping with him again. Oh, and when they met again, she didn't tell him she had moved from LA to Chicago.

"While she was with him, she called to check on her daughter, who was staying with us. Unfortunately, we were at the ER with her because the little girl broke her arm."

"She still did not tell him about the baby?"

"Nope."

"I think she planned to tell him when he called, but he never did and she's moving on."

"That's sad."

I am sweating as I sit still; these two women are no doubt talking about Ciara and me. The odds of this seem almost impossible. Here I am, waiting to take this long flight, hoping to run into her, while her best friend's fiancé is sitting right here.

"So, she gets pregnant from the same guy twice and can't tell him?"

"The interesting part now is the guy she is dating just asked my fiancé about proposing to her."

I will not let that happen. Oh my God, I am about to be a father of two and would have never known. Now I want to have her locked up as much as I love her. I lost a child, and yet she still did not feel a need to tell me.

"I don't get it; why would she not tell him? "Doesn't he have a right to know?" the black lady asked.

"I said the same thing. But I can't ask too many questions, remember Steven is only telling me in pillow talk."

"Oh, I get it, but she needs to tell this guy."

"I agree, but she doesn't want to bring drama to his doorsteps?"

"She has given the child her last name."

"So, what is the guy's name?"

"Steven won't tell me, and she hides the birth certificate of the girl who I must say is just beautiful. Let me show you pictures." The brunette reached into her purse and showed the other woman the picture of the little girl on her phone.

I have to do something. The only way I can find her is by befriending this lady who will lead me to her.

I got up and walked up to the ladies. "Hello, ladies."

Six

PHILIP

Hold on Philip; let me get this straight. Are you telling me I have a granddaughter and you're about to have another child?" my dad asks, surprised.

"Yes, that is exactly what I am saying."

"Of all the women who have falsely said they had your child or children, why isn't the woman with your actual child or children willing to reveal herself? I don't get it."

"I don't get it either; she feels she is being selfless by allowing me to have a life I do not want with Hillary."

"Son, what are you going to do?" He throws the question at me.

"I am heading to Chicago to get my children and their mother, or should I say, my family." The answer suddenly became unequivocal. I smiled.

"Do you have pictures?" Dad asked.

I reached into the envelope filled with all the information about Ciara and Filipa, brought out a picture of both mother and daughter, which I handed to my dad.

"She is a beauty, and so is my granddaughter, and what is her name?" he asks, pointing to my daughter; it sounds strange just thinking that.

"Are you ready?" I chuckled.

"She named our daughter Filipa. She's a woman with a good sense of humor; I have to say." I've had my moment alone of pride and joy at the knowledge of my daughter, plus the fact Ciara named our daughter Filipa. I love it.

"Let me know what you need; I will support you all the way. Don't worry; I will keep your mother out of this and get Hillary away from you," he assures me.

"Thank you, Dad. I am not sure how I am going to react when I see my daughter for the first time."

"Just let your heart guide you, and you will figure it out."

"I still can't believe Ciara will have my baby and not tell me. She didn't even try to reach out to me." I then remembered her telling me about my philandering.

"Give her a chance to explain herself before you jump to any conclusions. Granted, there shouldn't be an excuse for her behavior, but listen to her. You do not want to be in a custody battle. So, be reasonable when you get there."

"Thanks, Dad, I'll call you with an update once I speak with her."

Arriving at the suburban house, my informant had given me a weekly rundown of the day-to-day activities of Ciara.

Parked a few houses away, I watch Ciara from afar and feel the urge to grab her. I watch as she straps the little girl into the car and kisses the man before letting him drive off. I waited a few minutes before pulling into the driveway, just as Jimmy John's delivery guy did the same. I paid him for the sandwich and headed to the door and pressed the doorbell. I could hear her yell, "I'm coming!" I held up the Jimmy John sandwich she had ordered to the peephole so she wouldn't see my face.

She opened the door and stretched out her hand with money to me. Instead, I grabbed her hand and pulled it towards me.

She then opened the door wider. The moment she saw me, her eyes widened, and her body fell limp. I rushed forward to break her fall, scooping her up in my arms and placing her onto the living room sofa. I shut the door with a swift kick and darted off to the kitchen for a cool cloth for her head.

Seven

Philip

As she comes to, she tries to sit up quickly, but I held her down.

"Easy dear."

"How did you get here?"

"Airplane and car."

"Stop it, you know what I mean. How did you find me?" she snaps.

"Oh, that wasn't easy, but I found you, and I will say, with luck on my side."

I moved to give her room as she pushed her way to a sitting position and grabbed her sandwich. She talked and ate at the same time. A new Ciara, I said to myself. I watched her devour the sandwich. She was probably starving and tired, which explains her feeling faint.

"You can't be here; you have to leave," she said once she had devoured the sandwich.

"No, I do not," I responded confidently. "You and I have to talk."

"No, we do not; you need to leave," she jumped right up.

Standing up and moving really close to her, she tries to move away, and I pull her to me. I wrap my arms around her. Once our lips met, we were ripping at each other's clothes so fast. I took her right there on the living room floor and penetrated her quickly without thinking. I had to have my fill of her, not that I could ever get enough.

After a passionate session, we laid panting next to each other on the floor.

"Oh shit! Shit! Shit!" Ciara said, jumping up. "You need to get dressed, and you're leaving right now."

"No, I am not."

"Yes, you are. Now get dressed, please. We don't have much time."

"I will get dressed, but I am not leaving."

"Fine, let's start with that." We both got dressed, but she refused to look at me.

"You have a nice cozy place here."

"Thanks, and you need to leave right now."

"Ciara, I am not going anywhere."

She looked at the clock and I could see the fearful look in her eyes.

"How about we meet somewhere, or you come back another day?"

"No, I want to meet my daughter today and don't you dare lie to me because I know."

She stood there, speechless. I watched as stares at me in shock. Her eyes widen and she wraps her arms around herself.

"What do you want?" she asked, trying to put up a brave front.

"I want my family."

"I'm sorry I can't give you that. You are engaged to be married. I can promise you; I will never tell anyone about her if that's what you are worried about. Your future wife will never know about Filipa," she says fearfully.

I laugh, though her words hurt my feelings. Laughter was all I had to cover up my hurtful emotions.

"Is that what you think I am here for? I don't care if she knows. If anything, I want her to know."

"What?" her apprehension clearer now.

"Ciara, I am here for you, Filipa, and my child that is growing in you."

"No, no, no, no... this can't be happening; I am with James," she looks to me pleadingly.

"Believe it, it's happening," she shivers, and I pull her and sit her on the sofa just as the bell rings.

I went to answer the door. Standing with my daughter is Ciara's fiancé, James. Thanks to her friends, I already know all about him: thirty-two years old, went to high school with Ciara, never married, dated a few ladies, and was once engaged, but the engagement was called off three months later. He has remained around Ciara since she moved back to Chicago. They started dating a few months back, but he has never spent the night, which is something I still wonder about, as I have had Ciara in my bed a few times already. He and Ciara's best friend have a housing construction business. He's tall, probably 6'1", not heavily built, but still toned.

We immediately sized each other up. I'm confident that I can take him. "Hi," I said, holding the door wider to let them in.

"Ciara, we are home," James called out as he walked in carrying my sleeping daughter on his shoulder.

Ciara must have come out of her shock, as she gets up and takes Filipa from him.

"Thanks, James. Did everything go fine?"

"Yes, she had a great time. That's why she knocked out."

"Ok, thanks, can we talk tomorrow?" she said to James, but he didn't move.

"I'll wait for you to put her down while I make tea." We all stood in awkward silence.

"Hi, I'm Philip Webster. Filipa's father," I state, breaking the awkward moment. The shock is written all over his face as I grinned.

"James. Ciara's fiancé," he responded with confidence that made me squirm. Two can play this game.

"Excuse me," Ciara said, obviously not sure what to say as she watched the standoff. She takes Filipa to bed as I walked back to the living room.

James followed me and took a seat, watching me. We stare each other down, and I know this is territorial; I can sense he feels it's his territory.

Ciara returns looking mortified when she sees us. "Hi James," she says to him, avoiding eye contact with me.

Giving me the grin of the chosen one, he gets up and pulls her into his arms, deep kissing her in front of me.

If only I could throw it in his face that I had just made love to Ciara a few minutes ago before he came, but I could see Ciara blowing my brains out if I said that, so I just stood there and watched. It took a lot for me not to punch him. I will let him have this moment and no other, I firmly tell myself.

Once she breaks the kiss, she pulls him to a corner by the door. "James, I am sorry about our night being cut short, but I need to speak with Philip alone please," she said with a strained face.

"Ok, I will be here in the morning," he said, kissing her cheeks.

"Thank you." She closes the door, then goes to turn off the whistling kettle.

"Philip, let's get to the reason you are here over with so you can leave."

"Ciara, I am not leaving without seeing my daughter."

"You saw her; she's sleeping."

"I am spending the night, so I can see her first thing in the morning," I calmly state.

"Did the Webster's millions dry out so that you can't afford a hotel for the night? Sorry, you can't spend the night here," she sighs. "James is going to be here first thing in the morning. How do I explain you spent the night to him?"

"I don't care about him. You need to break the engagement with him anyway."

"I don't need to do any such thing."

"Oh yes, you do Ciara; otherwise, you wouldn't have made passionate love to me less than an hour ago, and I am sure he doesn't know you are pregnant again with my child."

"I am not pregnant; whatever you heard was a false alarm, and us earlier was a mistake."

"Since you want to play hardball, I would be happy to tell him, and I can call my lawyers right now and tell them to start preparing the custody papers for Filipa and get a court order for a DNA test of your pregnancy."

"You wouldn't dare do that, why would you want custody of Filipa? What will your fiancée say?"

"She's my daughter, and why wouldn't I want custody of her?"

"Can we work something out?"

"There's nothing for us to work out, Ciara; I want custody of both children and you as my wife."

She laughs in my face. "Wife! You have really lost it. We both know you like your life traveling the world with Barbie dolls clinging to your arm."

Her words fueled the anger I was holding back. "There you go deciding what I want for me again; you didn't think I had a right to know I lost a child, that I have a living one, and that you are pregnant again with my child. Even after the passion we shared. I cannot believe you would do this to me. I have broken my engagement with Hillary so stop deciding shit for me without asking me first," I let out, raising my voice.

"I am sorry, I didn't want to bother you plus..."

"Bother me?" I yelled. "Bother me with knowledge of my children? Are you out of your mind?"

"No, I just thought it was best."

"You thought it was best and took the joy away from me, and you were going to do it again, had I not found out. At what point did you think you would tell me about my daughter? When she graduates from high school or when she's ready to get married? Tell me, Ciara, when?"

"I am sorry, I actually thought it was best." Her voice breaks. "I really am sorry, Philip. How did you find out?" she asked quietly, disheartened.

"A little birdie told me."

"Please just tell me how you found out."

"A little birdie called your best friend's fiancée."

"What! Vivienne told you? How did you two meet?" Her questionable expression said it all.

"She didn't know who I was while she was busy yapping away about you."

"How? I don't get it?"

"Well, I was taking the same flight from LA to Chicago, hoping I would run into you again. After the wedding, I found out you had left your workplace, but you had told me you take the same flight to Chicago every so often, and I figured I'd stay on the same route in hopes of seeing you again. I did not know you'd moved to

Chicago, but I guess I now know why you didn't tell me about your move. Vivienne was telling a friend about you. I just listened as she talked. It sounded too familiar, but I didn't want to believe it until she mentioned your name. It all sounded too good to be true, so I started talking to her." I paused. "Got her information. Tracking you from there on was easy."

"Ugh, I always told her she talks too fucking much," she groaned.

"Ciara, why did you leave the room in LA? I thought we'd expressed so much to each other."

"My maternal instinct woke me up, and I called Steven and Vivienne. They told me they'd rushed Filipa to the hospital with a broken arm. I left you a note with my contact information and waited for you to call me for weeks. I kept checking my phone. I thought things were great, and I would have told you the next morning about Filipa had they not informed me about the broken arm. When you didn't call me, I realized I had to move on, so I accepted James' proposal," she said, her voice shaking.

"You didn't think I needed to know about my daughter? I still can't believe you didn't tell me about her and her brother; children you and I created out of pure passion and..." I stopped, turned my back to her, my anger slowly abating, but the hurt still gripping me.

"I wanted to tell you, but when you told me about the two women, I figured it was best not to tell you. It would have crushed me if you doubted me."

"I don't get it. You know for sure she is my daughter." I turn back to see her doubtful face.

"I didn't want you to doubt me since I had told you I couldn't have a baby, and here I was pregnant with twins. My only proof was I had not slept with my ex for at least two months before then, so I knew the babies were yours. At first, I was more shocked at being pregnant, then the reality of my pregnancy sunk in. Initially, I made no attempt to find you, and the first time I saw you after our night, I was about five months pregnant. You were walking into a restaurant with a brunette. I was surprised to see you and thought about coming to you, but you and the brunette wrapped around each other. I just felt it was best I went home and not let you see me. Truth be told, my hormones were raging that day, and if you had seen me, which I was sure you would have, I probably would have poured all the craziness on you that day. To save us both an embarrassing moment, I just drove home that night. After that day, I couldn't find you, and when I did see your face again, it was on a magazine detailing your elaborate engagement to Hillary, your fiancée.

My not telling you Filipa was not intended to hurt you; I honestly thought it was best, and I am truly sorry."

I sighed, realizing that my philandering had cost me knowledge of my children. My father had always warned me about it. God help me, I can't even remember the woman she is referring to. I have been all over town with different women. I wouldn't know who she saw me with.

"I don't even want to imagine how much Vivienne told you," Ciara said, breaking into my thoughts.

"I had to charm a lot out of her," I responded with a grin. We remain silent.

"Since I can't convince you to leave, we can at least have dinner, and you can sleep in the guest room," she stated.

"I need to be near you, Ciara."

"Not going to happen, Philip. It's best we don't confuse things; I need to think clearly about everything without mixing sex; we need to have a plan from here onward."

"Point of correction, Ciara, I only make love to you." She blushed.

"I made lasagna earlier today. Would that be ok?"

"That should be fine." We walked to the kitchen, set up the table, and started eating in silence.

"Tell me about Filipa," I asked, and I noticed that made her smile and put her at ease.

"She's a happy child, very stubborn and friendly. She's, of course, a Disney channel fan. A Minnie Mouse lover. She loves to wear boots and loves coloring."

"How was the pregnancy with her?"

"Well, there were two of them, so it was very uncomfortable sleeping or moving around. I moved here six months into the pregnancy, so I could be around family and get more help."

"Your family lives around here?"

"Yes, my sister, Stella, lives just five miles from here; Steven and Vivienne are 2 miles from here. My cousin and parents live close by, too."

"That's great. She has family around her."

"Oh yes, all the attention spoils her, already showing her diva side," she chuckles.

"How is business?"

"Very good. I'm glad I can do what I love and still be able to spend time with her." I could see the joy in her face.

"How is this pregnancy?"

"I don't want to believe I am pregnant. I think my period is just late so I am going to give it a few days. I am trying not to think about it," she states mildly, but I could see the anxiety in her eyes.

"Why?"

"I am engaged to James, who I have not been intimate with, so if I am pregnant again, it would be from the same man as my first child. A man that is engaged to another woman."

"I see that as a good thing."

"What part of all that I have said is a good thing?"

"Well, the part about me being engaged is incorrect and the part about you being pregnant rings joy in my ears. It also tells me I'm not wrong about how we feel about each other. You should break up with James; I would suggest you tell him soon because if he tries to kiss you again as he did earlier, I won't sit back and watch. And about my ex-fiancée, she found your information before I did, ripped it up, and threw it out the window. Is the reason I didn't call you. I broke up with her that morning because of that, but she has refused to get the message and is still wearing the ring." I paused to make sure she heard I broke up with Hillary.

"I can't just break up with James," she said in a low tone, though the words were forceful.

"Why not?" It seems easy, far as I am concerned.

"Because I like him and we have plans, plus I had convinced him I wanted to wait before we have any intimacy and two months ago, while dating him, I slept with you. I have always wondered, did the condom break, and you didn't tell me?"

"Yes, one condom broke, and I didn't see a need to tell you because you had told me the first time we met you couldn't get pregnant."

"I thought so too the first time until I kept falling asleep at work and was always tired. I went to the doctor, and she said congratulations, you are pregnant. I was thunderstruck. I was happy, of course, but I struggled with telling anyone. Then my grandmother died, and I decided to move back, knowing I would need help with the twins. Finn was a such a beautiful baby." She wipes her tears. "My consolation is the fact that I still have Filipa, but the pain of losing him is still there." She sniffles.

"Imagine how I felt when I heard my son died from a casual conversation between two women."

"I am really sorry," she said, wiping more of her tears.

"I wanted to tell you in LA, but when you started talking about the two women, I figured it was best just to stay quiet."

"Did you ever think and feel that I deserved to know?"

"Yes, I just didn't know how to tell you because I didn't want you thinking I am forcing a life you don't want on you."

"Ciara, from the moment I saw you at the airport, I wanted more with you. Granted, I didn't know what the more was, but now I do. I want a life with you and our children. I can't let you marry James. I know you don't want to marry him, otherwise you wouldn't have had sex with me today."

She chuckles. "What is it about you that I can't resist, anyway?"

"I don't know. I guess it is the same with me. I can't resist you either. Please Ciara, give us a chance." I plead.

"You will have to give me some time. I waited for you to call. When I didn't hear from you, I accepted James's proposal and we already have plans laid out."

"Make it quick. I certainly did not enjoy watching him kiss you, and I have a feeling he will keep doing that whenever he sees me with you."

She nods.

We cleaned up and returned to the living room. We talked more about work. Ciara showed me her designs and projects she is working on. The intelligence of this woman blew me away. "Let's go to bed; I will get sheets for the guest bedroom."

"Ciara, I need to hold you tonight."

"Phil, I don't think that's a good idea. You know we won't just sleep."

"I promise no hanky Panky. I am quite tired."

"Ok, be warned, Filipa might crawl into bed at night."

"That would be great."

"You say that now until she kicks you in the face."

"I'm actually looking forward to it." I went to grab my bag from the car.

"You came prepared."

"No, I came straight from the airport. I couldn't wait any longer."

We locked up, then checked on Filipa, who was sleeping beautifully. Then off to bed we went. Ciara goes to the bathroom to change, while I change in the bedroom. She came out wearing sleeping pants and a T-shirt.

"Is that how you go to bed?" I asked.

"No, but I don't want to entice you."

"You realize, try or not, I am enticed."

"You promised."

"Yes, come to bed." She leaves the door ajar.

"Why are you leaving the door open?"

"So Filipa can walk to me easily."

"Ok," I said. We got in bed, and I pull her to me. "Phil."

"I just want to hold you, Ciara."

We fell asleep until Ciara pulled out of my arms, slightly waking me up and placing Filipa between us. Though sleepy, my heart warmed when the baby's soft hand touched my cheek. Filipa then started slapping my cheeks. At first, I was startled; I then saw her beautiful brown eyes. I sat up and pulled her into a hug. She's friendly, just as Ciara said.

Ciara walked out of the bathroom, fully dressed in jeans and a T-shirt. "She needs to be changed; I am going to bathe her before she cries for food." She picked Filipa up.

"Can I come and help you?"

"No need, I got it."

"I know you do, Ciara, but I want to be a part of it."

"Ok, come on. You can pick her clothes for today. Look in her closet over there."

I went into the room, then the closet, picked out a pair of purple, flowery pants and a matching blouse. The happy child was now ready for her day. After her bath, Ciara puts her in the highchair for a bowl of cereal.

Ciara's phone ringing interrupts our family breakfast.

"Hi, James," she says.

That name brings a frown to my face. Why the fuck is he calling this early in the morning?

"No, I will stop at Stella's place later in the day."

There was a pause while James answered.

"Can we talk about that later?"

Another pause.

"Ok, I will see you later. Ok, thanks, bye."

She walks back to the table. "Phil, when are you leaving?"

"I don't know, but what I know is I want to spend the day with my daughter."

"The plan was to spend the day at my sister's place, a family cookout, and I don't think it's your kind of scene."

"When did family not become my scene?"

"James is going to be there."

"So am I."

"Philip please. Let's not turn this into a battle."

"I am not backing down, Ciara. James doesn't get to spend the day with my child while I stay in a hotel room. I am coming with you. Unless you want me to begin a custody battle before we talk."

"Don't threaten me, Philip. That will not work; otherwise, you will find out just where Filipa got that stubbornness from," she stated forcefully.

"Fine, but I am still coming with you. I leave Monday morning."

"Are you seriously trying to be cheap about a hotel?" she teases.

"Call it whatever you want. I am staying and spending time with my daughter and you."

"Ugh! I hate you so much right now," she scoffs.

"Yes, I know how much you hate me when you scream my name when I am inside you,' I volleyed back.

She stands behind Filipa and gives me the middle finger, then walks around to Filipa, "Filipa honey, say hi to daddy."

"Daddy!" she said with excitement.

"Yes, I am your daddy." It seemed like a newfound word to her. She kept repeating daddy. Daddy. Daddy. Over and over. Almost as if she was confirming to herself that I am real.

"Whoa, you sure know how to charm the ladies. Even your daughter is charmed," Ciara says.

"I'm the charmed one," I said as I leaned in to scoop Filipa out of her chair. She screamed with excitement and let out the best giggle ever. I needed to bond with her in the time I had left, so I played with her as much as I could.

Before leaving for the barbecue, I called my dad back. He had texted me a few times, wanting to know the outcome of my visit.

"Hi, Dad."

"Hi, Phillip, how are the children?"

"Child, and she's fine, and there's no doubt Filipa is my daughter."

"That's good news. And Ciara?"

"That is another conversation. She is engaged."

"What? How are you going to handle it?"

"Not sure yet, but I will figure it out."

"Ok son, be careful and think before you act."

"I will, thanks, dad."

"Please let me say hi to Filipa soon."

"Ok."

I will not let her be alone around James when he still thinks they are engaged, and I need to spend more time with my daughter before I travel for business. I know I want Ciara in my life, but her independence and stubbornness are giving me a run for my money. James in the picture really makes it harder.

We arrived at her sister's house, which was close by. I guess she had told them I was coming with her. Everyone was quiet when we walked in. Filipa let go of my hand and ran into the room. A Ciara look-alike walked up to me. Some of her facial features were more prominent, but no doubt, they are sisters.

"I am Stella. Ciara's sister."

"Philip Webster, nice to meet you."

"Are you the Phillip Webster of the hotel chain?"

"Yes."

"Holy shit, no wonder my sister refused to tell us your last name; she just said 'Filipa's father is coming, be nice.' We were shocked because she had refused to tell us about you, so when she firmly said to be nice, we all just kept quiet."

I chuckled. I am discovering how much of a complex woman Ciara is.

"Come in, let me introduce you to everyone," Stella said.

I walk around, meeting everyone. I met Ciara's parents. Her dad is half white and half black, her mom looks biracial as well. I can't place her mix, but I can tell what an older version of Ciara would be. Beautiful.

Just as we're all settling in, Steven walks in with Vivienne, who looked shocked to see me.

"Nice to meet you again, Vivienne."

"What are you doing here?" she asked.

"I am Filipa's father."

"What!"

"I am sorry I didn't tell you all the while when we met, but thank you."

"Steven is going to kill me."

"You're damn right I will," responded Steven. Then he turned to me. "Oh hi, I am Steven."

"Yes, Ciara's best friend." That's going to take some getting used to, I thought, because Steven looks like he and Chris Hemsworth could be identical twins. "I am Phillip, that giggling little girl's father." I was getting entertained with more information about Ciara and how wild she gets when watching football. They all joked about how she's usually the only woman in a room full of men. I could not imagine my ever-ladylike Ciara yelling with men. They all laughed that I should prepare to see the other side of her. I was enjoying my surroundings until James entered. The moment he saw me, he pulled Ciara into a hug. I got up right away.

Ciara mouthed 'please' to me. She doesn't let him kiss her. By nighttime, Filipa was asleep as I carried her to the car. I overheard Ciara asking James if they could talk tomorrow. I didn't hear his response, but I saw her walk back to the car.

I tried not to bring it up as we headed back home. Once Filipa was put to bed, Ciara and I sat down to talk.

"Phillip, lay out your plans for me."

"I want my family; I want to marry you and come home to you."

"Are you ready to give up your life in LA? Because I am not moving back there."

"Then, I'll move here."

"What happens when you tire of the life here?"

"What makes you so sure I will ever tire of a life with my children?"

She shrugs. "It's just the fact that I don't see you being the playdate-daddy kind, and this is not a part-time thing. It is forever."

"I'm fully aware of that, and I want it all with you, granted we will need a bigger house than this, and I will travel from time to time, but I want to come home to you and our children."

"Before we talk about marriage, why don't we try to work out how you will fit Filipa into your life and schedule, then we move from there."

"I can live with that, but you will have to break that engagement before I leave."

"You need to give me time on that."

"I will give you until Wednesday."

"Maybe." I want to challenge her answer, but I decided not to.

"When do you have to leave tomorrow?"

"I have a meeting at 11 am; I have arranged for a pickup at 10 a.m."

"Filipa goes to daycare tomorrow. Steven, James, and I have a consulting meeting at 11 a.m."

"Why are you in a meeting with James?" This does not sound good to me. The sooner she breaks off this engagement, the better I will feel.

"James and Steven are the contractors on my project."

"So, you work with them?"

"Not always. I had to bring James and Steven in on this project."

"I understand. It's your business, but our lives cannot truly begin until you break up with him."

"Phillip, you cannot just walk in here and tell me what to do. I accepted his proposal and for me to return his ring, I need to be sure I am doing the right thing. So, I need time. He has been very good to me, and we laid out our plans, which I was happy with. You can't just walk in and expect me to throw all those plans away."

"Wednesday, Ciara, or I tell him you and I have been together intimately, and you are possibly pregnant with my child again."

"Don't you dare do that," her commanding tone was unwavering.

"Oh, I dare, Ciara, you gave me that right when you with-held knowledge of my children from me. Wednesday, and that's it."

"Gosh! I hate you, Philip Webster."

"Yes, I know you hate me when you moan my name," I said, pulling her to me. She fights in my arms, but once our lips touched, we tear each other's clothes off again. Why she keeps fighting this insane attraction, I do not know, but I do know I will not let her marry James.

Monday. I open my eyes to see her beautiful face. "I love waking up next to you," I mumbled to her.

"Don't get used to it."

"Oh, I will get used to it, because it is our destiny, Ciara, whether you like it or not."

"Just get out of my bed, Phillip. Go so I can think, please."

"Make sure part of your thinking involves breaking up with James."

Over the next couple of weeks, I tried to visit my daughter more and get closer to Ciara. I learned she is a hard-working, stubborn, and a very independent woman, but she still found time for us to talk every day about Filipa and other stuff. And when we're not together, we spend hours on the phone talking to each other. The more we spoke, the more I fell for her, and the more I missed our time together when we were apart.

Jealousy always rises in me whenever she mentions James, however. I realized that he's not an easy beat as I'd thought. He's winning the stable guy card in Ciara's eyes while I still look like the non-fatherly or non-play-date dad, as Ciara says.

Every moment we get alone, I use it to remind her how sexually compatible we are, as much as she refuses to admit it. We willingly come into each other's arms, and her face lights up whenever I return from LA. She plays it cool, but I noticed she takes time to look good for me. I appreciate her effort, but I love it when she's without make-up and wearing a simple T-shirt and jeans with her hair in a braid. On those days, she's more beautiful than ever, even though she doesn't think so. I let Filipa remind her she's beautiful.

Eight

Philip

Mr. Webster, there is a lady on the line. She said her name is Ciara, and she is on her way here to see you; she would like to know if you have a few minutes to see her."

"What are you sure? She said Ciara, and she's here in LA?"

"Yes, sir. She said if you are too busy, it's okay and she doesn't need to stop by."

"Let her in, and in the future, never hesitate to let her in." I'm surprised Ciara is coming to see me. I talked to her last night, and she didn't mention coming to LA. Why is she here? I sure hope she is not coming to say something ridiculous, like she is moving forward with marrying James. I choose to believe she has a good excuse to be here and not to deliver bad news to me.

I was still in a cheerful mood awaiting Ciara when Hillary waltzes in like she owned my office. I should have told my PA to never let her in. I want to throw her out, but I also want to know what stupid stuff she has up her sleeves. She is still wearing the engagement ring, knowing I'll never marry her.

"Hi honey, I was in the neighborhood, and I thought I'd drop by for a moment with you," she said in a tone that sounded more like a screeching sound to my ears.

"Hillary, what do you want? I'm rather busy and I have a meeting in a few minutes," I responded in a steely tone, hoping she will get the message.

"Phillip darling, I just want us to talk about our lives together."

Oh no, she did not just drop that bomb. When is this woman going to get the message that I have no feelings for her? "Let me stop you right there. There is no life or togetherness with us. Frankly, there is no us." I emphasized the last phrase in a commanding tone. She chuckles like I hadn't said anything important.

"Come on Phillip, you know we are a perfect pair," she said as she walked closer, dropped her bag on the chair, and moved behind the desk to me.

"I know that day you were upset, and I was upset too, but I forgive you. Can we please go back to being us, what we used to be?"

Does this woman realize how upset and annoyed I am with her?

She bent over, trying to give me a view of her breasts in her tight dress.

I turn a stern look. "Are you serious? Is this the best you can do?" Before I could say more, her lips were on me, trying to force a kiss. I shoved her off me just as I heard the voice.

"I apologize for interrupting, I was just in the area, and your PA said I could come right in," Ciara says calmly.

I jumped right up. I could see the stunned look on Ciara's face. Knowing her, she will not speak to me again if I don't salvage this moment. I can already read her look of disbelief, I bet her overzealous mind working faster than Einstein to prove her theory that I'm still with Hillary and she needs to stay with James.

"Ciara, you are not interrupting. Hillary here was just confirming our dis-engagement by returning the ring, and she was just leaving." I turned a stoned face to Hillary. Talk about thinking on your toes. She looked at me, then at Hillary's stunned face as Hillary moved to pick up her handbag.

"Oh, sorry about your dis-engagement. I was just in the area."

"Please don't be sorry, Hillary and I have both concluded that amicably canceling our engagement is best for us." I walked around my desk to Ciara, pulling her further into the room, and called out to my assistant, who raced in. "Ms. Hillary was just leaving; can you please see her out?"

Hillary had shock written all over her face. Nevertheless, I was glad Ciara saw Hillary walk out. The door slammed as Hillary left, and of course, she did not leave the ring. Hopefully, she finally got the message, though.

Ciara moved closer to my desk. She is beautiful, I thought, even in her simple outfit. She was just wearing a plain white blouse and jeans that hugged her hips, sneakers, hoop earrings, and she had her hair in a pony-tail.

"I didn't mean to disrupt you guys. I was just in the area, and I thought to say hello before I head to the airport."

"First off, you disrupted nothing. Second, what are you doing in LA? Third, why didn't you tell me you were coming, and fourth, why are you on your way to the airport?"

She chuckled at the way I had listed all my questions. "I got the hotel contract yesterday evening. They called me late last saying they wanted me to meet with a rep and see a particular work done here in LA, so they asked if I could make a day trip here today. Their call came in after we had talked, and I decided not to call you about it since you said you were going to a business meeting. With the amount the company is paying me, I couldn't refuse such an offer, plus I saw it as an opportunity to see Amy, but she is out of town, and so is Claire. Stella is watching

Filipa for the day, and maybe for tonight if anything weird stuff happens. But since I was able to view the site and finish the meeting earlier than planned, I just thought I'd say hello to you before I head to the airport. I hope I answered all your questions."

"You certainly did," I responded, grinning. "Since you are here, which is a pleasant surprise by the way, why don't I take you out tonight, and we can both catch the flight out to Chicago tomorrow?"

"Phillip, I can't spend the night. I didn't book a hotel room."

"You can stay with me."

She gives me her signature questioning look. "Really Phillip? Stay with you when your fiancée just walked out here like she was going to return with a shotgun? Did you not notice how angry she was?"

No human standing close by could miss the venom and anger oozing out of Hillary.

"Ex- fiancée, and I have a spare bedroom. Come on Ciara, we can hang out in this fun city together and be in Chicago first thing in the morning. Plus, our daughter is in safe hands. Ciara, one night in LA together."

"Phillip, I just stopped by to say hello because I have a few hours before my flight."

"One night in LA together, just us hanging out."

"I thought we did that at the wedding."

"We stayed in just that building, but what I am asking is that we go out to a restaurant together."

"Didn't we do that the first night we met?"

"No, we didn't have a choice in the restaurant that night, either. Tonight, we get to choose. Come on, Ciara."

"The choice of a restaurant is a bogus reason," she chuckles. "My only spare change of clothes in case I am stuck for the night is another pair of jeans and a T-shirt, nothing fancy."

"My dear, you will do just fine in what you are wearing."

"You are making me second guess my stopping by to say hello."

"I would have never forgiven you if you hadn't stopped by, and I find out later that you came to LA and didn't call me. I am still a little upset you didn't tell me you were coming."

"Like I said, it was an impromptu trip."

"Make it up to me by letting me take you out tonight."

"Fine, let me inform Stella that Filipa will spend the night with her."

"You can do that on our way out."

"We don't have to leave right now, do we? Don't you have to work? I can keep myself busy while you finish."

"I am not busy when you are in LA. Let's go."

We stopped at my favorite restaurant. One thing is for sure, whenever Ciara lets down her guard, she is the most amazing woman to hang out with. She had lots of stories to tell of her and Steven in high school and how most people thought they were dating.

"I have always wanted to ask, how come you two never dated?"

"Honestly, it wasn't like we didn't try, considering we were always together and are still together. However, we kissed once when we were in tenth grade, and boy, was it horrible. From then on, we decided our friendship was more important, plus we both had crushes on different people at that time."

"How come I'm just now hearing about a kiss between you two? No one else has mentioned it."

"Aside from Steven and I, you are the only other person who knows. Could you imagine if Vivienne found out with her blabbermouth? So, if it gets out, rest assured I will kill you," she said, running her index finger across her neck.

"Scouts honor. It stays and dies with me, but rest assured, I will tease you about it."

"As long as Steven doesn't know that you know."

I feel better now knowing that Steve and Ciara got any potential feelings out of the way. If I'm being honest,

I have been struggling with him being so close to her. Though I could always tell he truly loves Vivienne, I had always wondered, given the slightest chance, if he would make a move on Ciara. I can put those worries to rest now, thankfully.

I told her about Hillary, and how we had dated since high school. At first, it seemed logical, since our mothers are close friends, but as I grew older, I realized she wasn't the woman for me. Unfortunately, she is still stuck on the image of us together more than her future happiness.

"Are you sure it is just the image? Maybe she is actually in love with you."

"Trust me, I know Hillary is not really in love with me. Once Hillary finds a guy she can present and fits into her social class, she would instantly be in love."

That got a laugh out of Ciara.

"What do you want, Phillip?" The question came as a surprise, but it was an excellent opportunity. I know she asked in a subtle tone, but whatever answer I give, she is going to take it seriously. I leaned back in my chair and maintained eye contact.

"I want a life with you and more children with you, making a mess all over the house, and all of you welcoming me home every time I walk through the door. I will tell you it never gets old whenever Filipa runs to me to welcome me. I want to wake up next to you every day. Bottom line, I want all of you and then some more children with you." I gave myself a pat on the back for not missing a beat and noticed Ciara broke eye contact. I have certainly cornered her.

"What do you want, Ciara?" I ask, putting her on the spot.

"Nice try, Phillip," she says, trying to avoid the question.

I'm not ready to let her off the hook. "Come on, Ciara, you can tell me. Your secret is safe with me." I smirk.

"Fine, I want the same things as you, only I am a little skeptical about giving into that want right now."

"Why are you skeptical?"

She gave a sarcastic chuckle. "I walked into your office a few hours ago, and you were kissing your fiancée."

I knew this was coming. It was just a matter of time.

"She was kissing me, not the other way around, and I seem to recall that I put a stop to it even before I knew you were there."

"Yes, but the fact remains she is wearing the engagement ring you gave to her around town, and every magazine still refers to her as your fiancée. Much as I want the same things as you, I have to face reality or the possibility of you and Hillary getting back together. Just where does that leave me if I allow myself to give in to the thought of a life with you? To be honest, if you two are really not together, as you so often claim, why is she still wearing the ring?"

I am happy she wants the same thing as I do, but I must admit, she is right about Hillary wearing the ring. Certainly not about the possibility of us making up, however.

"Hillary, as I told you, is not just an ex-fiancée; she is also a childhood friend. Our mothers are close. I don't want to embarrass her publicly and announce the engagement is off. I want to give her that chance to say it. You and I both know if I announce our breakup, she will lose face in her group. I'm a nice guy, but she and I are over. I broke up with her the morning after the wedding when she threw your information out. The only person who has a key to my apartment after that day is my father. I urge you to give us a chance and not hold the fact that I am being nice to Hillary against me."

"Ok," she consented.

Since I am on a roll, I might as well put my bid in. "When are you going to break your engagement with James?"

"Nice try Phillip. For now, James stays as long as Hillary is still wearing your ring and announcing it to the world."

I sighed, knowing right there she is driving a hard bargain. She is making me request the ring back from Hillary, and I know right now that Hillary would never willingly give the ring back. "Fine, do I have your word that you will break things off with James once I get Hillary to announce our broken engagement?"

"You have my word that I would consider breaking things off then, but right now, I am not even considering it."

"As much as I want to fight that, tonight, I get to spend time alone with you, so I won't fight."

Ciara laughed at my words.

Once we left the restaurant, we drove around a little before stopping at a sports bar, since Ciara had to catch the football game. I thought the night was for us to bond, but once Ciara got into cheering at the sports bar, I was forgotten. I sat watching her enjoy her beer and cheer for her team. By the time the game ended, a few guys thought they had a chance with her. It shocked them when she declined their advances by saying she was at the bar with me. I got a pleasant chuckle from that. As always, she is oblivious to how easily she attracts men. By the time we arrived at my apartment, she was totally herself.

We sat and talked all night, laughing all the way until the moment I kissed her, and from that moment on, we made love to each other repeatedly. At no time did she fret that I did not wear a condom. This I was very glad about because I fully intend to get her pregnant again. Maybe then she would see we were meant to be, and not James.

We woke up a little late the next morning. She had to call Chicago to reschedule an earlier meeting. I thought she was going to be upset, but she seemed pleased to be with me. We had breakfast before heading to the private plane for our trip to Chicago. Ciara was a little hesitant about the private jet. However, once seated, she loved it. We talked all the way to Chicago. Arriving in Chicago, I had my driver take her to her meeting, and I went straight to my meeting.

After a night with Ciara, I feel on top of the world. I'm pumped and ready to take on the day. I realized I need to find a place in Chicago, but I am hesitant about buying a place so soon and potentially having to sell it.

Truly, once Ciara breaks up with the dumb guy, I plan to move in quickly and convince her to marry me. Buying a house for us will be next, as I'm sure she would prefer a house as opposed to a penthouse. I could start looking for something bigger in her neighborhood. Maybe that will convince her that I am here to stay. To be honest, I would prefer we move back to LA, but to have Ciara in my life, I would move anywhere.

If I start looking in her neighborhood with her, I can also convince her to go looking with me and let her pick the one she likes and decorate the house as she pleases. I can almost see her getting all excited about decorating a room for Filipa.

And that will also give me more time with her. The more I can take her away from James, the better I will get at convincing her to break up with him.

After my meeting, I contacted a local realtor about wanting a bigger house in Ciara's neighborhood. I might as well get the ball rolling.

Ciara texted me later in the day, telling me about her whole day. It was so unexpected but very nice to know what she did, and I am happy she is including me in her day. I will see Filipa tonight. Better yet, I can convince Ciara to go out to dinner with me. It would be an excellent step towards getting her to continue to see more of us together and less of James.

Nine

Philip

A week later, I stopped by to pick Ciara and Filipa up as planned for my dad's birthday party in California. Of course, there was a big angry bear called James about to get into his car, but the moment he sees me, he stops and growls at me.

"I know you fucking did this."

"Did what? I just got here," I responded calmly, though I am fully aware of what he's talking about. It's more fun to play dumb.

"Quit playing dumb with me; you think I don't know this trip to California is a ploy to get Ciara away from me?"

I chuckled. "You really think Ciara going to California for work and meeting a legend in her field that she has always wanted to meet is a plot? Tell me, what are you afraid of?" I asked, smiling, knowingly messing with his head.

"I am afraid of nothing; I just don't want you to hurt Ciara any more than you already have."

I burst into laughter. "You really think I hurt Ciara? You are delusional."

"I have to leave because I can't stop her; neither can I watch her leave with you," he retorts.

"Yes, please leave; I assure you Ciara is happier with me than she is with you."

"Funny." He feigns a laugh. "I am the one she's engaged to, not you."

I seriously want to punch him for reminding me. "Not married, just engaged. Until that status changes to married, she's fair game. Might I remind you she and I share a child; therefore, we will always be involved." Yep, I played my ace card.

"We will be married soon," he said, his fury palpable.

"Like I said, until that day, she's fair game."

"Fuck you, Phillip; I will not get into a brawl with you because of Ciara, but rest assured, she will be my wife." He finally gets into his car and speeds away.

I stood there watching him. If only he knew Ciara was screaming my name, just a few hours ago as I pounded into her. And I know she hasn't been in bed with him since the so-called engagement. Like I said to him, she's fair game until they are married, if that ever happens. I need to prove to Ciara that I am dependable, and flying around the globe for work doesn't mean I won't be there for her, Filipa, and any other child we will have.

Maybe knocking her up again wouldn't be a bad idea. I was bummed when she told me that our escapades after the wedding did not result in a pregnancy, but I aim to make it happen every chance I get.

I pressed the bell. Filipa opened the door, and I scooped her up in my arms, making her scream with laughter and joy. It never gets old.

Ciara comes down with their suitcases. "I think we are ready. We will be back Sunday night, right? I have a client meeting on Monday morning."

"Yes, ma'am," I agree, smiling.

"Be serious Phil, I can't afford to miss the meeting," she stated matter-of-factly.

"I assure you, Sunday night, you will be back here, and we will all have had a good time."

"No hanky-panky Phillip, I mean it."

"I can't help it if you find me irresistible." I grinned. In response, she mouthed, "Fuck you. "

"Yes, I know, that's when you scream my name," I smirked.

We arrived in California; I was beyond happy to introduce Ciara and Filipa to my family. My first stop was my sister Maggie's house. She had been expecting to meet them both. Maggie, my dad, and Henry are the only ones excited about Ciara and Filipa. Everyone else, including my mom, all felt Ciara was after my money, and that I should still marry Hillary and not care about Filipa. They said Ciara is engaged to another man, so Filipa should be his problem.

Much as I am excited about this weekend, I must make sure I keep Ciara away from the venom of my mom and Hillary. She must not know what they think, because God knows that would only drive her into the arms of James, and I would be damned if I let her marry him.

My sister Maggie and her husband Cameron opened the door with their very excited little girls: my nieces. After they introduced themselves, Maggie got Ciara to talk about her work. Ciara's excitement when she spoke of her designs was mind blowing!

After that, Maggie showed her around their home so she could make suggestions about colors and style. By the time we were ready to leave, Maggie and Ciara had their own mom coded language. They had exchanged phone numbers and cooking recipes, along with tips for how to raise little girls. My sister pulled me aside and said, "I couldn't have asked for a better sister-in-law. Make sure you don't screw this up and you guys make beautiful babies."

"Don't worry, I won't screw things up. Thanks for welcoming her."

Filipa was sleeping by the time we arrived at my apartment.

Ciara was surprised to see I had created a little girl's room for our daughter. "This is awesome, Phillip. I absolutely love the décor! I can see her getting all excited when she wakes up. When did you do this? Must have been right after I left here, right? I mean, it's so nice! I am legit, impressed by the work. It's a true princess's room."

Then, I showed Ciara her room, though I was truly hoping she would spend the night in my bed like she did the last time she was here. As soon as Filipa was tucked in, we sauntered to the living room.

"I really like your apartment. It is very modern and nice, but still not the best for a little girl."

"I can change it just like that," I say, snapping my fingers. "If you want to move here, that is."

"I can't move here, Phillip, I like Chicago. My family is there, and our daughter would get to grow up like a girl, not a little diva. Besides, what about James?"

The mention of the name lights a raging fire within me. "Ciara this weekend, can we not talk about him at all?"

"Fine, just know that when I am making decisions like that, I have to consider him." She looked away and changed the subject. "So, this building you wanted me to look at. Can we go and see it before the party?"

"Sure, that would be a good idea."

I went and poured us a drink and we sat in my living room watching TV. I had downloaded a few of her favorite chic movies; she gave me a cheerful glance when she saw the list. She finally settled on Serendipity as the pick for tonight. We sat next to each other as we watched the movie, and by the time the movie was over, she was snuggled next to me. I couldn't help but pull her closer to me. She mumbled, "Phillip."

"Yes."

"Take me to bed." Not wanting to give her a chance to clarify her request, I picked her up and took her to my bed, where I plan to make sweet love to her. She barely stirred as I removed her tee shirt and pants. The sexy lace underwear she had underneath was enough to get me ready for her. I climbed into bed with her.

Just as I was about to pull her close to me and sleep, she says, "Kiss me Phil."

I didn't wait to think if I imagined her saying those words. I just smashed my lips with hers. We made love so slowly that I felt my soul was merging with hers. By the time we were done, I smiled to myself as I realized I didn't use a condom, and she didn't complain. She is not on birth control, that much I know. So, there is a chance if we keep trying, I could get her pregnant again. Gosh, I want more children with this stubborn woman.

Afterwards, she just stirred and cuddled next to me. By the time I woke up, Ciara was not in bed with me. I jumped up. I am not about to have a déjà vu day where she would be gone. Not bothering to put on my pants, I ran out, shouting her name. She responded right away, and then I heard the giggling sound of Filipa. It suddenly occurred to me that I am naked. I ran back to my room to get dressed.

I returned to join mother and daughter having breakfast. It was a beautiful sight. We sat as a family to enjoy our breakfast.

But just as we were cleaning up, I heard a loud bang on my door. Who could possibly be banging on my door this early? Only my family knows the access code. With today being my dad's birthday party, we are all expected to be at the house. Not sure what to expect. I asked Ciara to take Filipa to another room. I went to answer the door, and it is my mother and Hillary standing at my door, both looking devious. They tried to come in; I blocked their path.

"Philip Webster, will you move out of the way so I can come in?" my mom commanded.

"Sorry mom, now is not a good time," I calmly replied.

"You can tell that tramp to leave, and I hope you are not planning on bringing her to your father's birthday party tonight."

"First off, no one is leaving, and does Dad know you are here?" That question brings a shocking look to my mom's face. Hillary is unusually quiet. She's letting my mother take the lead.

"I am going to close the door and do not bang on my door again unless you want me to send security to come and remove you."

"You wouldn't dare," said my mom.

"Try me, or better yet, maybe I should call Dad."

At the mention of my dad, my mom squirmed and said, "Let's go Hillary and Philip. This is not over. Whatever hold she has on you, I will break it."

"Mom, that is what you are not getting. I am the one happily chasing after her. See you at the house, and Hill, stay the fuck away from me. If I see you talking to Ciara tonight, there will be consequences." She just stood there, shocked by my words. Surprised I am onto her.

"Bye." I close the door. Why my mom was adamant about Hillary and I was beyond me? I stood there in silence, trying to process what had just happened, but Filipa's laughter snapped me out of my trance.

I went to Filipa's room to find her playing with Ciara. "Hi, I hope we didn't cramp your style with your visitor."

"No, it was just my mom; she was in the neighborhood and wanted to remind me not to be late tonight," I lied. I couldn't possibly tell her it was my mother and ex-fiancée who came to try and kick her out of my house.

"Ok, anything you need help with?" she asked.

"No, just a few phone calls. Can you excuse me a minute?"

"Sure, Filipa and I will finish up here."

Once I closed the door to my study, I called Dad to let him know about Mom and Hillary. "Dad, you won't believe Mom came here with Hillary, prepared to throw Ciara and my daughter out. I have had enough of this. I will not marry Hillary, and I don't care what social class she belongs to."

"Not to worry, son, I will have a word with her. How are Filipa and Ciara?"

"They are fine."

"Great, I can't wait to meet them!"

"Sure dad, see you later."

I went and got ready for the building visits I had promised Ciara. We dropped Filipa over at my sister's house and drove to the buildings.

The building tour took longer than I expected because Ciara wanted to take some pictures and asked lots of questions about texture of some materials used in the design. I was worn out by the time we returned home.

I arranged a car to bring Ciara to the party since I had to be there early, and she was tired after the tour.

At my childhood house, my mom had a few fuming words for me about her visit and why she was still adamant Hillary is the woman for me, as though we were in the 16th century, and we had to forge a marital alliance.

The truth is, Hillary's family would gain much more from such an alliance than mine, but it would make my mother feel more powerful in her own social circles, since it will give her important connections. It was truly selfish reasoning, so I had to nip her act in the bud.

"Mom, if you do not want me to publicly announce my disengagement to Hillary and my engagement to Ciara tonight, you will stay away from her and put an end to the nonsense you and Hillary have planned for tonight. "

"You wouldn't dare make such an embarrassing announcement," she sneered.

"You and I both know that Dad and I have never cared about your social groups. So, for me, it is not a threat but something that will bring me much joy; if anything, it will finally make Ciara believe me because right now, with a ring on Hillary's finger, she finds it hard to." I paused, letting my words sink in.

"Fine, you have my word; your pretty tramp will not be hung publicly."

"No more name-calling, either. She's the mother of your grandchildren, and she is certainly not a tramp, but a very hardworking, smart and beautiful woman."

"Children!"

"Child for now, but I intend to make it children."

"Oh, my! Tell her I said this is not over."

"I will not deliver such a message. Now smile, because your social friends are arriving, unless you want me to speak louder about Ciara. "

"We have a deal, Philip," she says begrudgingly.

"Good, glad we understand each other," I turned my back and walked away before her annoying group could stop me and start asking about my never-happening wedding to Hillary.

I sat next to my dad. "I do not want to imagine what you said to your mother. She looked like she was going to pass out," he says with a chuckle.

"A few words, like the announcement of disengagement to Hillary and engagement to Ciara," I jokingly say.

"No wonder she looked like she saw a ghost, congrats. Did Ciara say yes?"

"No, I wish that woman wasn't so independent and stubborn, but she will, I guarantee it."

"Make sure she says yes." He leaves just as Henry showed up.

Henry and I got into our usual banter for a while until my sister brought Filipa to me. I set Filipa up on a chair next to me, and she seemed happy with her big bowl of ice cream.

I hear Henry speak foully. "Check out that woman in the blue dress standing at the entrance. God spent extra time on her. She's a beauty. The way her hips are sway-ing is making my cock twitch."

"What the hell, man? My daughter is here."

"Oops, sorry, not used to a pretty little lady in our midst."

"Anyway, I'm waiting on Ciara, not interested in your clan of beautiful women."

"You keep waiting, the sexy one is walking towards us. Thank God I wore proper underwear. I can almost come just looking at her."

"You're a crazy man," I say as I turn to look toward the woman that has my best friend acting weird, only to find that the woman is Ciara, in a blue dress that molds her body perfectly. The deep V with sheer fabric creates intrigue. Though the dress and the sleeves are long, the deep V and the front slit that shows her leg as she moves draws attention. Her full hair and perfectly done make up enhances her striking beauty.

I immediately gripped his arm tight. "That woman is Ciara, so you'd better wipe off any inappropriate thought going on in that head of yours. God help me if you so much as look at her inappropriately, I'll break your face."

He tried to remove his arm, but I held on tight. "You can't be serious; she doesn't look anything like her pictures. The one you showed me didn't do her justice; I would have moved to Chicago long ago for her," he said, enthralled by her.

"I mean it, Henry, wipe out every inappropriate thought from your head." I let go of his arm just as Filipa jumped down from the chair, screaming, "Mommy!" I pulled Ciara close to me and kissed her cheek. "You are stunning," I said to her.

She just smiled as she looked at Henry.

"Ciara, meet my best friend Henry, and Henry, this is Ciara Kellington."

She gave him that smile that would melt any man's heart as she stretched her hand for a handshake. "Hi, Henry, nice to finally meet you."

I watched Henry drool over Ciara. "Hi Ciara, the pleasure is all mine," he held on to her hand longer than usual as I tried to pull him away. "Phillip, can you get Ciara a drink, please?"

"No," I responded, pulling Ciara's hand from him. "Ciara needs to meet some people."

As I attempted to walk away, Henry whispered in my ears, "I can tell you right now man, I am not the only man here drooling; you need to look around you. You should have made sure she wore a different dress."

I did a quick eye sweep, and Henry was right; most of my so-called friends, I could tell, were ogling her. I felt like shouting 'snap out of it, haven't you all seen a woman before?' But Filipa tugged at my hand, so I held back. I then turned my attention to her and instinctively held onto Ciara's hand to make sure no one pulled her from me.

"Daddy…"

"Coming dear, let's get you a drink, and mommy is coming too."

"You two can go. I will wait here," Ciara said. I pulled Ciara closer to me and whispered to her. "If you wanted me to allow you a free roam tonight, you should have worn a different dress. Since you didn't, you're stuck to me all night."

"I can wear whatever I please, Philip."

"You are coming with me, or we leave the party, and you change out of this dress."

"Whatever, let's just go." She moves past me.

"Good, glad we reached an understanding."

"Don't count this as a victory. I just didn't want to make a scene. People were staring at us," she says.

"Correction darling, lots of men are having nasty thoughts about you, and the women with them want to choke you, just so you know," I state matter-of-factly.

She responded with that familiar, defiant look. This woman is really a force to be reckoned with, but I'll take my win.

After we got our drinks, I took her over to officially meet my parents. I made eye contact with my mom, telepathically reminding her of our earlier conversation.

"Ciara, my parents, Carter and Holly Brewster."

"It's a pleasure to meet you; you have a lovely home," she says to my parents.

"The pleasure is ours," my dad responds, as he shakes Ciara's hand. "And thank you for my lovely granddaughter, also sorry to hear about the loss of the boy."

"Thank you."

"Nice meeting you Ciara. Have we met before? Where did you go to college? I am guessing you didn't go, right?" asked my mom, not hiding her disdain towards Ciara.

My intent was to pull Ciara away, but much to my chagrin, she responded, "I don't think we've met. I'm sure I would remember Philip's mom and my daughter's grandmother. I graduated from the Art Institute of Chicago, and I also studied as an exchange student at Politecnico de Milano in Italy. I used to work here in LA, but I currently run my own design company in Chicago."

I could tell my mom didn't expect that answer and tried to hide her defeat by raising her glass for a drink.

I noticed Hillary heading towards us. I tried to pull Ciara away again, but it seems my mom had pulled a string in Ciara that wasn't meant to be pulled.

Ciara would not move; instead, she turned to my mom. "Did you study art as well?"

Hillary arrived just in time to save my mom from responding; she barely graduated high school, but she always seems to define everyone by their social status and not what they had to offer intellectually or otherwise.

"Philip darling, everyone is asking about our wedding date," Hillary said, smiling as she took a sip from her glass. Then she noticed Ciara and almost choked on the drink she'd just sipped. "Uh... Uh... Hi."

"Hi Hillary," Ciara says.

"I didn't recognize you; you clean up well. I guess with the right amount of cash, just about anyone can change their look from street to semi class," Hillary cattily remarked.

I wanted to slap her and defend Ciara, but knowing Ciara, she took control. "I certainly agree with you on that, with the right amount of cash anyone can be nipped and tucked, but you know what, no amount of plastic can clean up low self-esteem because I believe Philip mentioned to me a few hours ago that you two broke up months ago, and yet, here you're still asking about a wedding date. Or did I hear you wrong, Philip? The fact that she can't handle the breakup is why you've not officially announced the disengagement, right?" Ciara says, turning to me.

"That's absolutely correct, and we can clear up any confusion here tonight by making an official announcement since most of our friends and family are here, right Hillary?" I asked. She stood there stunned, not expecting Ciara to speak up. I smirk at her. "You shouldn't have tested Ciara," I telepathically say to her.

My mom quickly interrupted. "That announcement wouldn't be necessary tonight, Philip; I think Hillary gets the message. Please excuse us," she said, pulling Hillary along with her.

My dad turns to Ciara, holding her hand in both of his. "Never, have I met a woman that stumps my wife. I'm so glad Philip met you. I would love to see your work sometime," he says with a smile.

"I'm sure we can arrange that, Dad," I responded for Ciara. Feeling pride bubble up within me towards Ciara for scaring away Hillary and my mom, my hand rested possessively on her waist.

"That would be great," Ciara responded, smiling.

My dad walked away, leaving the two of us alone.

"I'm sorry Philip, I didn't mean to mess things up for you and Hillary. She just got me upset."

"Look at me."

She looks.

"I am thankful that you said those words to her and my mom. They both had it coming. Anyway, now that we are squared with Hillary, is my marriage offer accepted?"

"The deal was for her to return the ring or announce the dis-engagement. That hasn't happened yet."

Damn it, she's right. But I'm a lot closer than I was.

"Come on, let's meet some of my friends before we all sit for dinner. Then I can take you home."

"Philip let's not get ahead of ourselves here. Your sister has agreed to take Filipa home with her, and Amy will be picking me up later tonight. I may not return until the morning."

"Nice try Ciara, just so you know, the only bed you'll be sleeping in when you're in LA is mine, and I know you'll kill me for what I'm about to tell you, but I canceled your arrangement with Amy. Tonight, is my night. Amy can have another night, but not tonight."

The shock on her face speaks volumes. We stared each other down as the music and the surrounding crowd drowned out. She lets out a sigh before speaking.

"First off, I do not appreciate you rearranging my schedule. Second, I would let you have tonight just because I wasn't really interested in the men Amy had lined up for me. Third, don't count this as victory because I may be interested tomorrow, and tonight is all about your dad's birthday. That's the only reason I'm letting you have all these wins."

In all she said, all I heard was the lined-up men. "What men Ciara?"

She responded with a wicked smile. "Now, hotshot. That's for me to know and for you not to find out."

Just then, Henry arrived beside her, and Ciara linked her arm with his. She smirks at me. I'm not sure which one of them to attack first.

"How about that drink, Henry?" she asked.

He didn't ask my permission; he just took her away. I decided he's the one to attack and I'll deal with him later.

I'm not too happy about Amy arranging blind dates for Ciara. The last time Ciara was in LA, she'd told me Amy wanted her to go clubbing with her, but she'd turned her down. But now it sounds to me like Amy wants to hook Ciara up.

Guess Amy is going to be seeing me at every outing she has with Ciara whenever Ciara is in town.

Ten

Phillip

After my dad's party, Ciara seems to let down her guard. We talk for hours every day about Filipa, her work, and just about everything. She tells me more about her likes and dislikes, and she gives me the full details about her trip to Italy, something I didn't know about until she'd mentioned it to my mom.

I also now have an apartment in downtown Chicago, since Ciara had shared her full schedule with me. My apartment became our love nest. She would stop over whenever Stella could watch Filipa, and we practically jumped each other at the door each time. Sometimes we would catch a movie or just take walks and spend time together. For once in my life, I became a one-woman guy.

Henry called me crazy the day I told him I was flying to Chicago just so that I could spend four hours with Ciara before heading to Boston, but at no point did the journey seem long to me. Ciara was always the focus. That trip confirmed how much I'm fucking in love with

Ciara. Seeing her that evening as she walked in, she had obviously missed me as much as I missed her. She came prepared with dinner and discussion of her work. When she walked into my apartment, I was so happy to see her. I started kissing her right from the door. Later that night we caught a movie.

Just as we were leaving the movie theater, a male voice called her name. We turned to the voice, and I heard her say, "Kevin, what are you doing here?"

They hugged, but his hands were rubbing her body in a way that drove me nuts. Kevin is her ex-boyfriend, so I know he has seen Ciara naked. That did not sit well with me.

I pulled Ciara away from him.

Ciara was startled but said nothing; she introduced Kevin and I to each other.

"I've moved back to Chicago, Ciara; maybe we can hang out sometime."

"Oh, sure, my number is the same. Call me, maybe we can."

"Cool, see you later," he said before walking away.

My anger was building. Why the fuck is Ciara planning a date with her ex-boyfriend with me standing next to her? "What the fuck was that about?" I asked.

"That was me being polite; I have no interest in going anywhere with him; we were done before we broke up; he was probably just trying to be polite."

"He can shove his politeness up his ass, and I don't want you anywhere near him."

"Oh my, Philip Webster, are you jealous?" she teased.

"Damn right I am, especially the way he was holding you, like he was getting a feel of your body."

"He did not!"

"He did, and that's not acceptable. I don't want you near him."

"Ok, fine."

I was shocked she agreed. I was ready for our usual argument. I took my win, and we went towards my apartment building. We spent the rest of the night making love. When we slept, I whispered to her, "I am so in love with you." The next morning, as we happily walked out of the building, we bumped into one of the few ladies from my past.

"Philip Webster, what a surprise."

"Hi, Tiffany."

Before I could say more, she had her lips on me. I pushed her away, but the damage had been done.

"Oh, Philip, don't be shy, I'm sure your lady friend here knows she's only temporary, we can pick up from last Saturday in LA right baby," she purrs as she moves closer, but I instinctively move out of her reach.

I could read the vengeance in her look, but Ciara's face was one I didn't want to read because it was almost in tears. I'd broken and disappointed her. I knew her thought process right away, and I knew she'd think I cheated on her.

What really happened was that I had canceled our date last weekend because of work, and Henry and I had ended up at a party after work. There, we ran into Tiffany, who had tried to ride home with me, but I'd turned her down in front of the guys, which must have bruised her God's-gift-to-men ego. Now, she's taking her revenge.

"Lousy liar," I said.

She laughed. "I'll see you in LA," she says, walking away.

"Ciara, I swear to you, she's lying. I turned her down last weekend."

Not a word from Ciara.

"She's lying Ciara, please say something."

"I'm almost late for my appointment. I need to go," she says and walks away from me before I could recover from what had just happened. She got in a cab and left.

I called her later, but she refused to talk about it. Instead, she made us talk about Filipa. The Ciara wall was back up again. Damn you Tiffany, I mentally yelled.

The next two days, getting Ciara's wall down was difficult. I had to stay on task with her at the end of our call; I had to face the issue. "Ciara, I didn't sleep with Tiffany, she's just upset I rejected her."

"I know you didn't; I was just a little irritated by how far women will go to be with you. I don't know if I have the strength to fight them. Hillary is still wearing your ring just to stay attached to you, and Tiffany was lying about sleeping with you. Who does that? I mean, it's all just weird, and there were the women you said lied about you being their baby's father. Really, it is a lot for a woman like me, Philip."

"Marry me, Ciara, and send a message to them that I am taken."

"We had a deal, Philip, and your end of the deal is not fulfilled yet. "

I grunt, knowing she's right. I'll let it slide for now. At least she trusts me.

Eleven

Ciara

My phone ringing shows Philip. I have an inward smile, though I keep a natural tone as I answer. "Hello."

"Hi, Ciara."

"Phillip, I am a little busy right now. In a few hours, I am going to have over 20 kids screaming around my house."

"That's what I am calling about."

I pause mid-stride. What has he done now? I stood still, waiting for the next shoe to drop.

"The planning crew will be there in about 10 mins."

"What planning crew? I didn't hire anyone. I want a small birthday party for Filipa."

"And I want my baby girl to get all her princess wishes."

"Just spill it Phillip. What have you done?" I scoff.

"Bouncy castle, clown, Disney princesses, catering party, and some decorations. Don't blame me; I just took ideas and suggestions from my sister, so blame her."

"You have got to be kidding me," I said, my tone harsher than I intended. I held the phone away from my ear and let out a few grunts. Phillip just keeps piling on the disqualification records. "How much is this going to cost?"

"All paid in full."

"This is exactly why you and I cannot work out. I said small party and instead of discussing with me, you send a circus. What am I going to tell James?"

"What does James have to do with this?"

"We are engaged, and he loves Filipa, so we discuss like adults."

"So what?"

"How do I explain the elaborate party to him? He's going to feel blindsided."

"Ciara, you're not married yet, and Filipa is my daughter, not his. I can throw a lavish party for her as I please," he yells.

"You love to throw that at him, don't you?"

"Not my fucking problem if he can't handle it."

I can sense the exasperation. "You're not even going to be here for the party; I don't get why you had to send this circus," I say to him, maintaining my calm even though I am upset with him.

"Who said I won't be there?" I can hear the sudden delight in his tone.

"Aren't you in New York?"

"Was in New York. I just landed in Chicago. Should be there in an hour. Just a quick stop at my apartment to change."

Just what I didn't plan for. I can tell he's happy to throw me a curveball.

"Are you really coming to the party, Phillip? I thought you said you wouldn't be able to make it."

"Well, Filipa is more important, so I am making it."

"Fine, just make sure you behave yourself."

"Will try my best is all I can say. See you soon Ciara, bye."

I had to call James right away since he was about to pick up chairs from my sister's house. I let out a few breaths to calm myself as the phone rang.

"Ciara, we are just loading the items into the trunk. We should be there shortly."

"I am sorry, James, change of plans. Phillip has just called me saying he has paid for a party planner, and they are coming with everything we would need."

"What? I thought you told him it was a small party."

"I certainly did, but he just called me about a princess party planner coming with everything we need."

I could hear the grunt of annoyance. "Ok fine."

"Thank you, please come back. They should be here shortly."

I could tell he was upset, but he let it go. Phillip was certainly not making things easy by always throwing the fact he's Filipa's father in James's face.

I need to find a way to make this all stop. I am still upset from last week's incident with the woman Tiffany. I want to believe Philip, but my smart mind keeps reminding me he's a player, and he cheated on Hillary. What makes me think he won't do the same with me? His expression when that Tiffany woman spoke about their weekend was that of shock, but he told me he went to a party afterward with Henry. Only, he didn't mention her. I heard him when he had said he was in love with me and I saw her mischievous look, but the reality is Philip is a player. If not Tiffany, then who did he spend the weekend with?

Thirty minutes later, the party planning crew arrived with tons of materials meant for an elaborate party. It had me in awe as they set everything up, much as I hate to admit it. Filipa was beyond happy when she saw everything, too, from the princess tables to the bouncy castle, the popcorn machine, and the table set up for face painting. They even came prepared with goody bags that put the ones I made to shame.

By the time the guests arrived, everyone was blown away. There were as many servers as party guests.

Stella came to me. "Much as you refuse to admit it, Phillip certainly blew your mind with this party for Filipa," she says.

"What he did is throw money around and I dislike it whenever he does that," I scornfully replied.

"You realize, as her father, he also has a say," she counters.

"That much I know, but I dislike when he plays these games."

"Have you stopped to think maybe it is not a game, and maybe he truly wants to be with you? The man can barely take his eyes off you."

"I find it very hard to believe that he truly wants to be with me, when he is still engaged to Hillary and…" I keep quiet, not wanting to say more.

"I thought you said he had broken the engagement?" she asked, surprised.

"So, he says, but she is still wearing the ring all over LA as his fiancée, which is why I have to keep reminding myself to stay focused on James, and with time, whatever Phillip wants will fade."

"Guess the question is, do you want it to fade?"

I remain quiet, knowing that I don't. I stand next to my sister, silent, and I could not tell her that every single moment Phillip and I have had the chance, I have willingly made love with him. I truly cannot resist the guy, but women like Tiffany make me pause. Meanwhile, James is my stability. We work fine together, and he loves my daughter very much. He and I have known each other for a long time, too. By now, I know we can make a marriage work between us, and I know he loves me, but God help me; my heart is with Phillip, and it pounds every time he touches me.

"Ciara, you haven't answered me; do you want it to fade?" she asks again.

"We'll talk later. Filipa is running towards the gate." I immediately ran after Filipa, a perfect excuse not to answer the question since I couldn't think up a lie that would suffice. As I got closer to the gate, I saw Philip walk through and pick Filipa up. I turn around to see James frowning at the sight. Once Filipa was safely in her father's arms, I walked back to James, who immediately wrapped his arms around my waist.

That certainly earned a jaw-clenching frown from Phillip, who turned his attention to Filipa. I avoided saying much to Philip throughout the party. However, we both smiled for the camera with Filipa. My friends all had a few comments about Philip, which I completely ignored. They all seemed very charmed by him, especially Vivienne, who has now become his number one champion. I, on the other hand, made sure my attention was all on James, who was only too happy to return the attention.

By the time the party was over, all the children were drained of energy as they left. Filipa turned to James, who carried her to bed, and we tucked her in.

The party crew had cleaned up by the time I returned. Philip was talking with Steve, who was waiting for James since they had an outing planned. I could tell James did not want to leave once he saw Phillip, but he couldn't say that to Steve; instead, he pulled me into a passionate make-out session in front of Steve and Phillip. I lean into it, knowing it will enrage Phillip. I had to do this to get Philip to fade, or maybe to convince myself to feel more for James. I failed.

The kiss ultimately had no spark for me, though James looked like he enjoyed it. We said our goodnights, and I thanked Steve for coming.

Once the door closed, Phillip pulled me towards him forcefully.

" Don't you ever do that again," he growled.

"Do what?" I asked innocently, like I had no idea what he meant.

"You really want to play this game, Ciara? You willingly kissed him just to spite me, and don't think I did not notice," he continues in the same irate tone.

"All I know is I kissed the man I am engaged to, so I'm not sure what you're talking about," I reply with a smirk.

"He may be the man you are engaged to, but he is not the man your heart and body yearn for."

I laugh just to hide the truth of his words. "You flatter yourself, Phillip," I scoff.

"Do I?" The undertone in his words was not lost on me as he moved closer and cornered me into the wall. His closeness always throws me off my game.

"Thank you for the elaborate party for Filipa. I need to go to sleep," I say, succumbing to every last shred of power I have left.

"You're both welcome, and I know she had a great time," he whispers, leaning closer.

"Yes, she did. Can you move, please?" I request, making every attempt not to touch him or be moved by his titillating scent.

"I haven't touched you in almost three weeks. Not touching and feeling you is driving me insane. Is it driving you too?" He leans into me; I could smell the freshness of his every breath. I inhale his smell. I have missed his smell.

My body is aroused, but I choose to fight it. "No, it is not driving me anywhere. Rather, it is making me think clearly."

He laughs in amusement; he knows I'm lying. His lips collide with mine before I could think. At first, I refused to open up to him, but I couldn't fight it any longer. Our clothes are flying as we feed into our desire. We moved away from the door and made it to the sofa in my office.

Each movement, each thrust, made me scream his name more and more. I have missed him so much. I could never get enough of him. By the time we both came, I tried to get up, but he held me close to him.

"I missed you Ciara, please tell me you have missed me," he asked quietly.

I remain quiet. I know he won't let me hear the last of it once I confess the truth to him.

"Please, Ciara, just this once can you at least tell me the truth." His gentle tone and subtle request were my detriments.

"I missed you too," I said, grudgingly confessing.

He lets out a deep breath. "Thank you. That's all I needed to hear." He releases his hold on me. We dressed in silence, picking up our clothes from the floor. He pulled me to him again once we were dressed. I tried to pull out of his arms, but he would not let go of the hold.

"Your lips and body speak two different languages. Your lips speak no, and your body speaks attraction to me like a moth to a flame," he whispers in my ears. My eyes widen because I know he's right. I remain quiet, not letting the language of my lips utter a word.

"I have a plane to catch. That's the only reason I am leaving; I flew in just for Filipa's party. I didn't want to miss her birthday." He says, releasing me.

"Ok, where are you off to?" I asked, finding my tongue.

"Back to New York. I need to meet with some important people tomorrow. Then I have a busy week, and I might fly to LA for a day or two. I am not sure yet, but I will let you know. I will be back two weekends from now to see Filipa."

"You don't have to rush back," I say, trying to hide the disappointment I feel for his impending absence.

"I need to see you and Filipa every week. Why you choose to deny what we have between us, I don't understand, but I will be here every week."

"Don't you see Philip? We just cannot work."

"I do not see that, and I am not about to argue with you tonight. I will take my leave and call Filipa tomorrow morning on her iPad." He kissed me again before walking out.

I went upstairs to check on Filipa before heading for a shower. Once showered and seated in my office with my cup of tea, I looked through some pictures taken at the party.

Unexpectedly, my doorbell chimed again. I am surprised because I was not expecting anyone.

To my surprise, James was at the door.

"Hey, you're back so soon. I thought you guys were partying all night. Is Steve, ok?"

He didn't answer and just pulled me into a deep kiss. At first, I went along with it. I realized the kiss was getting longer, and he rips my pajama shirt open, my breast exposed. His hand grabs my breast, and he kept being rough.

I then struggled with him until I was out of his arms, not without slapping him. "What the hell is wrong with you, James?"

"I'm sorry for being rough, but can't you see how much I want you?" I see the rejection eating at him, but that's no excuse for his senseless action.

"So, you thought it is okay to be rough to get what you want? Just leave before you make this worse!" I yelled.

"Are you sleeping with him?" he yelled back.

"Who?" I asked, a little clueless.

"Philip are you letting him have what you are denying me?" he asked, raising his voice.

"I am going to pretend you didn't just ask me that. Get out of my house," I commanded in the calmest way I could manage.

"It is a simple yes or no Ciara," he quietly asked. His anger seems to have dissipated, but mine just began.

"What if I don't answer? Will you force yourself on me?" I sneered, then continued. "No, get out."

He finally walked out and slammed the door; he must have thought I answered no to the question he asked, but I meant no, I am not answering the question.

Once I locked the door, I started crying. I changed my nightwear. I was still sobbing when Phillip called on FaceTime; I answered without realizing how terrible I looked.

"Ciara, have you been crying? What is wrong?"

"James was here, and we had a fight," I sniffled.

"What about?" his face contorted.

"You," I say, wiping my tears.

"What did James say to you that made you cry?"

I remain quiet.

"Ciara, answer me, what the hell did he say to you?" he asks again. Though subtle, I could see the dreadful look on his face.

"Nothing, he was just a little..."I struggle to continue, still in disbelief that James would do what he did.

"A little what, Ciara?"

"Nothing..."

"A little what? Tell me."

"A little rough. He wanted to know if you and I've been having sex," I answer, avoiding looking at the camera.

"So, he got rough with you," he states.

"It was nothing. I told him to leave."

"Did he leave?"

"Yes."

"Ciara, you need to break this engagement, because if he hurts you again, I will break his nose. Tell him I said that."

"Philip..." I started to speak, but he cut me off.

"I don't want to hear any more excuses Ciara, since you are ok, goodnight."

I started crying more after he hung up, wondering why Phillip couldn't just understand my predicament. I lay in bed sobbing and could not fall asleep as I tried to find a solution to my chaotic circumstances.

Twelve

Philip

I received a call from a bartender about Hillary. He said she's drunk at his bar, and he can't let her drive home. The only phone number she gave was mine. Much as I know, picking her up is a bad idea. I couldn't just leave her there. After all, we were once close friends.

I arrived at the bar to find Hillary slumped on the table. She is totally out of it. My first instinct is to ask what the hell she is doing on this side of town, but her words are incoherent. Instead, I thanked the bartender and grabbed Hillary's purse before lifting her off the table. She was so out of it, she could barely walk.

As I drove, she continued to make incoherent sentences. "I caught him with her," "I am so not worthy," "you didn't love me, and he doesn't love me," "what is wrong with me?" "Why won't any man love me?" she rambled on and on.

I realized I had to find out where to take her. If I take her to her place, I will have to stay all night with her, but if I take her to my place, she can sleep in the guest room and I can lock my bedroom door; that way, her crazy self will not walk in on me naked. God knows a standing prick in the morning has no brains. I would hate to have to lie to Ciara about my involvement with Hillary, too. We've been slowly getting back together after the incident with Tiffany and James, and I know any slip up will erase all of that progress.

We had to stop twice along the way so she could empty her guts, but once we arrived at my apartment, I put her to bed in the spare bedroom. Then, I went to shower and locked my bedroom door. I don't want any surprises in my bed.

As I was getting in bed, Ciara called me. "Philip, I have been calling you."

"Sorry, I missed your call, busy night."

"Well, I just wanted to let you know. Filipa had a high temp today and cough, and before you rush over and rip my head off, it's nothing serious..."

"What! Is she okay?"

"She's fine now and sleeping. It is late. I just wanted to let you know before you get all upset that I don't share her care with you."

"Thanks, I appreciate that, but is she really, ok?"

"Seriously, you don't trust me? She is fine, her temp is down, and her cough is going down, too."

"Good, I will call her in the morning."

"You sound tired. I'll let you go. Not much sleep for me tonight. Filipa is in my bed, and you know she kicks." She laughs.

"Lucky her. She gets to sleep with you."

"Goodnight, Philip."

"Goodnight, Ciara."

I breathed a sigh of relief that everything went well. Glad Hillary is knocked out, too.

I woke up early the next morning, thinking I might have to drag Hillary out of bed, but she was already up and wearing one of my favorite t-shirts. I'm guessing she helped herself to the clothes in the laundry.

"Good morning, Hill."

"Hi Philip, thank you for last night. I don't even remember telling the bartender your phone number."

"You did, and he called me. Glad I was around and able to get you out of there. I had your car towed to your place, and I will arrange for a car to come and pick you up and take you home."

"Thank you. I truly appreciate it. I am sorry I had to dump all my shitty self on you."

"You are not shitty, Hill," I reply, which is the truth.

"Then why did you dump me for Ciara? And why did I find Jon in bed with another woman? What is wrong with me that men keep cheating on me? Please tell me, am I that terrible in bed?"

Boy, I am so not ready for this conversation. I need to call Ciara soon and ask about Filipa. But Hillary looks miserable. I can make this easy. "You are not terrible. Have you stopped to think maybe we are just the wrong guys for you? We cheated not because you are terrible, but we are just insecure and searching for something else. I think you just need to find yourself and meet the right guy. Until I met Ciara, I didn't think one woman was enough for me. Then, I met her, and she just blew me away. Now I don't want any other woman, I just want her. You and I were wrong for each other. I don't know what the story is between you and Jon. All I know is my cheating on you was not your fault. I was just searching for something which I found in Ciara."

"Thank you, Phillip. I think you're right. Once I get home, I'll send your ring back to you. Ciara is a lucky woman." If only Ciara would see it that way. The woman is so goddamn stubborn.

"Take your time and freshen up, and I will have trans-portation ready for you. I need to get ready for my day."

"Ok, I will stay out of your way."

I walked back to my room in relief. The moment I jumped in the shower, I realized I had left my phone next to Hillary. My shower had to be quick so I can grab my phone. Hopefully, no one calls me before I'm done.

Thirteen

Ciara

Filipa is feeling much better, and we can both call Philip on FaceTime. That should stop him from rushing over; the guy can act all crazy at times. She is a happy child today, no more temp, and her cough is still dwindling.

Nothing could have prepared me for the shock of seeing Hillary on FaceTime. I had to check again, making sure I didn't dial a wrong number.

"Hi Ciara," she said, all excited. She looked messy, like she just rolled out of bed, no make-up, and wearing one of Philip's favorite t-shirts. I don't need to be told she spent the night.

"Hi Hillary, is Phillip available? His daughter wants to talk with him."

"I think he's in the shower. I can let him know once he gets out."

"Thank you, bye."

"Wait, can I ask you a question?"

"Um… ok." What the fuck does she want to ask me?

"Why do men cheat?"

You have got to be fucking kidding me. Of all the most annoying questions in the world. "I don't know. Different reasons, I guess. But I know some men are unworthy of trust. I have to go now. Bye." I hung up without giving her a chance to say more.

How could Phillip do this to me? I begged him to leave me alone, but he refused and kept coming after me. He promised me he and Hillary were over, and stupid me. I believed him, even after the incident with Tiffany and the argument we had over James. I thought he deserved more than an iota of my trust because I know how some women can act crazy. I just wanted to be sure he really wanted Filipa and me in his life, but I guess he's an excellent liar.

He and Hillary are clearly still together, and I'm holding off on James, that loves my daughter and me, despite his last disorderly behavior, which he apologized profusely for. I have let myself get stuck on a cheating guy that is great in bed. I am so fucking done with him.

I switched my phone off. I don't want to hear from him today. I picked Filipa up and out the door we went. I cried on my way to Stella's house in disbelief that Phillip is still cheating. I had stayed out of James's arms for him. A great guy, who I almost broke my engagement with because of Philip. Well, no more. Once we arrived at

Stella's house, she knew right away that something was wrong with me.

"Ciara, you are crying. What's wrong?" she whispered, not wanting her husband to hear.

"It is nothing."

She snickered. "For you Ciara, crying means it's something. So, what is it?"

I let Filipa run into the house, and we both stepped outside where I burst into tears.

"Phillip is back with Hillary," I say through tears.

"Who's Hillary?"

"His supposedly ex-fiancée."

"What! Are you sure?"

"I called him on FaceTime before I drove here. She answered his phone, in his apartment wearing a favorite T-shirt of his. No doubt she spent the night with him."

"Are you sure? Maybe there is more to it," she says calmly.

"Why do you always defend him? I saw her. Only his father has a key to his apartment. The only reason she would be there is if he took her there, and I know Philip. She spent the night with him. She told me he was in the shower and asked me why men cheat. Why the hell would she ask me that if she is not insinuating something to me?"

"I don't know, sis; I just know that man loves you very much."

"Well, he can keep his love. I am heading to work. I have all Filipa's meds in her backpack."

"OK, please let him explain himself before you do something outrageous."

I drive to work, trying very hard to put away all thoughts of Phillip into a hidden compartment in my mind and turn my focus to work.

Fourteen

Philip

"WHY! Why the hell would you do such a thing?" I scowled at Hillary. "What the fuck is wrong with you?" I continued in the same angry tone. "You wanted to know why we are not compatible? Dumbass behavior like this is why we could never be compatible. Please get ready and leave my apartment. I thought we could remain friends and mend fences, but your stupid, selfish behavior would never let that happen. How could you have answered my FaceTime call knowing it's Ciara? Did you forget you are in my apartment, wearing my T-shirt without a fucking bra, and you look like you just rolled out of bed? What woman in her right mind wouldn't think you spent the night in my bed? What is wrong with all you crazy women?" I stood in anger, staring at her sad face. I can't wrap my head around her dumbass actions.

"I am sorry, Phillip; I don't know why, I just wanted to talk to her. I wasn't thinking."

"You're damn right. You have a clueless brain, and you had the audacity to ask her why men cheat? Are you fucking kidding me?" I couldn't hold back my wrath. Why the fuck in god's name would Hillary answer my phone? I wanted to help her. Now she has fucked me up really bad. I should have just sent her home and left her there.

"Phillip, I'm very sorry. Please forgive me. I can call her and explain to her, please."

I laugh at her words. "You have no idea how stubborn Ciara is. Her phone is switched off, and I know just how she thinks." I stared at her, wanting to toss the phone in anger, but I know better. "Damn you Hill, I was making progress with her, and you had to fucking ruin it."

"I will get out of your apartment. I'm very sorry. I didn't mean to ruin things for you, Phillip. I really am sorry."

I watched her walk away. Just how stupid could she have been? But I had no time to think about that, I had bigger problems on my hands now. For example, Ciara, Mrs. Stubborn, will not even give me a chance to explain.

Then, I had an idea. I called Stella, as I know Filipa would be with her today. That would mean Stella may have talked to her.

"Hi, Stella, is Ciara there?"

"She was here, but left for work. What the fuck did you do? She came here crying. I can't remember the last time I saw her cry like that. She said you are back with your ex."

"Shit, that's not true. It is all a fucking mix up."

"Thank God. I told her the same thing, but you know her. She is a mess, though she tries to put up a front."

"Where is she right now?"

"At a site with Steve and James."

"Fuck, she's with James?"

"Yes, at work."

"Ok, thanks, is Filipa better?"

"She is great and fully energized, a little cough, but she is good."

"Thanks a lot Stella, I have to try and get a hold of Ciara."

"Alright, I will tell her you called."

I hung up with Stella and all I could think about is how much I dislike Hillary right now. Like, why the fuck would she answer my phone? Now Ciara is with James, who I am sure is more than happy to make her happy. I know she wouldn't tell him, but Ciara can be an easy read for anyone close to her.

Hillary finally walked to the door, but I couldn't give a fuck about her.

"I truly am sorry, Phillip," she said.

I did not respond. I just turned around as the door shut.

Unfortunately for me, I have a crucial meeting today. Everyone was counting on me to close this deal. I had my head and mind in the game until Hillary fucked things up for me. Now, all I can think about is Ciara.

All day, I asked my PA to call her, but she must have switched off her phone. I tried Steve, but his phone was also switched off. I realized that probably wasn't the best idea anyway, as he is Ciara's bestie and would always take her side.

Henry stopped by my office later to discuss the meeting, but I could barely talk with him. He knew right away that my mind was elsewhere.

"Phil, what is going on? You were all excited about this meeting yesterday, and today you couldn't care less. What is going on?"

I took a deep breath before telling him everything.

He was speechless by the time I was done. "That's messed up. What are you going to do?"

"Fly to Chicago as soon as we are done."

"Alright, well, since you have to lead the meeting, I will take anything else I can off your plate."

"Thanks, man."

Right as we closed the deal, I could barely wait for the group to leave. I immediately grabbed my laptop and rushed out the door, straight to the airport.

I arrived at Ciara's house only to find out she wasn't home. Where could she possibly be? I went to Stella's house and found Filipa there. "Daddy, Daddy," she said, running to me; it never gets old the way she runs to me. I was thrilled to hold her and spend a little time with her. Stella told me Ciara is out with James and Steve and might not be back tonight, which is why she left Filipa with her.

My blood pressure shot to the roof the moment I heard that. Knowing her, she probably thinks maybe it is time to give James a chance.

"Can you please reach out to her for me? I have tried all day," I ask Stella again.

"I am sorry Philip, she made me promise not to contact her unless your daughter was in danger or had a life-threatening emergency. I guess she figured you would show up and try to convince me. I can't help you tonight, much as I would love to."

"Do you know where she went?"

"She did not tell me. All I know is she went with Steve and James."

"How are you supposed to reach her, then?"

"She got a cheap prepaid phone, and Steve's phone is working. She just told him not to answer your calls."

"Damn, she is so fucking stubborn."

"Stubborn is her middle name," she answers back with a chuckle.

"Please, Stella, I need your help. How do I fix Ciara and I?"

"Tell me what really happened."

I sat down and revealed everything to Stella, including how I had told Hillary to leave.

"I believe you Phillip, but my sister is the one that needs to believe you, and to be honest, I doubt she will believe you this easily. You know what they say, Love Has Many Faces. Jealousy and betrayal are two of them. Right now, Ciara is feeling both emotions and I honestly cannot tell you how she would react to this. I know she has been struggling with the idea of you betraying her. That's her biggest fear and with what just happened. You just confirmed that fear."

"All I am guilty of is helping a friend, please, Stella. How do I get her to see that I just helped Hillary out of a mess?"

"To be honest, I don't know. Maybe if Hillary herself tells Ciara the same story."

"That is easy; I will get Hillary to come and confirm my story to Ciara."

"Not so fast. Why don't you talk to Ciara first?"

"How?"

"You will have to stop by tomorrow morning."

"There is no way I would sleep tonight."

"Can't help you there. All I can do for you is let you into her house to wait for her, and I know she will kill me for that later, but that is the best I can do."

"I will take it; I want to be there when she gets home. I can take Filipa home with me."

"Not a good idea, you have obviously not seen the angry side of Ciara, so good luck when she finds you in her house," she says, shaking her head.

I knocked out on the living room sofa, but I quickly got up when I heard her arrival. Per Stella's advice, I have to stay calm once Ciara sees me. When she walked in and locked eyes with me, I watched her relaxed face instantly sour. Just like Stella said, I'm about to see a new side of Ciara.

"Hi Phillip, what are you doing in my house?" The words were simple, but the venom in them was potent.

"Hi Ciara, I came to speak with you about the misunderstanding that occurred yesterday."

"What misunderstanding?"

This woman is truly a force to be reckoned with. She is not throwing things, but I can still sense her anger emanating from her. I need to spit the words out quickly before she throws me out.

"Ciara, I know you spoke with Hillary yesterday when she was at my apartment wearing my T-shirt. I understand how it must have looked, but she was drunk the night before because she caught her boyfriend cheating on her. The bartender called me, and I couldn't leave her passed out in a strange bar, which is how she ended up in my apartment wearing my T-shirt the next morning."

"Great, I am glad to know you helped a friend, but you need to leave. James and I have a meeting with a wedding planner in two hours, and I need to get some stuff done before then." Her words stung like a bee.

The calm I was supposed to maintain flew out the window upon hearing the news. "Why the fuck are you seeing a wedding planner with James?"

"He's my fiancée, and we have decided to start planning our wedding, so can you go now, please?"

"No, Ciara, I'm not leaving. Why are you planning a wedding with James is what I want to know," I asked, not caring if I've raised my voice.

"I don't ask you who you are with, so I don't see why you are asking me why I am planning a wedding with a man I'm already engaged to," she spits out, the venom stinging me right in the face.

Just then, I realized that my anger isn't going to save the situation. So, I reined it in. "Ciara, please stop planning. I didn't have sex with Hillary. I can get her on the phone. She just acted stupid."

"Maybe you should have. What do you think James and I did all night?" she says calmly, though I could see the fire in her eyes, daring me to counter.

"What the fuck did you just say!?" Out goes my attempt to quell my anger. Now, my face looked disgusted by her words. I heard her clearly, but I wanted to make sure my ears weren't playing tricks on me.

"Did you have sex with James?" I ask again as my blood seethes within me.

"Not like it is any of your business what my fiancée and I do, but yes, we had a lovely time," she says with a smirk.

I didn't realize how fast I moved and grabbed her, pushing her to the wall. "Tell me you are joking, Ciara," I growled. When she turned her face away from me, I knew she wasn't lying. I stepped back from her. I couldn't believe she would knowingly hurt me like this. "Bravo," I say with a sad laugh. "You've finally succeeded in inflicting pain on me in a way I never thought was possible." I could not express the hurt I was feeling. Rather than say anything more, I simply walked out the door.

Fifteen

Ciara

I couldn't control the tears that rolled when I heard the slam behind him; he'd walked out without a fight. I am in pain as well. I'd wanted to inflict some of my pain on him, but now it has backfired. The hurt on his face would haunt me forever. Stella had told me what he said about Hillary, but my usual stubborn self was fighting against believing that was all that happened. I had gone out with James because I was madly jealous and feeling betrayed by Philip.

After dropping Filipa off, I went to work and drowned myself in the current project. To be honest, I've no idea how I managed to function throughout the day. By evening, when Steve and James asked me out for drinks, I'd happily agreed.

Lately, I'd found excuses to reduce my time with James, but with what happened yesterday, I'd no intention of going home to cry.

At the bar, I piled on the drinks. Steve tried to stop me, but I kept asking for more. I wanted to see the bottom of every bottle and glass, to the point I couldn't walk and found myself naked in James's bed today, which wasn't what I wanted. I have a vague memory of kissing him but completely blanked on if we had sex or not. Seeing him naked in bed next to me just confirmed my suspicion, even though I have no recollection of it happening.

Also, there isn't a wedding planner. I'd just made that up, and now I have hurt myself and the man I love deeply more, and even dragged James into our mess. He now feels more confident that we are truly together, all doubt regarding Philip, now erased. But I know damn well Philip is my everything, and I am pregnant with his child. I found out five days ago, and I've been trying hard to not tell him over the phone.

Oh, lord! I was so blinded by hurt and forgot about my pregnancy. Please, God, don't let me hurt my child. I desperately want this child with Philip. Oh God, what have I done?

Now sober, I have just added insult to my injury. The health of my baby, I pray, is not at risk with all the drinks I had last night.

Philip

I got into the car and punched the steering wheel a few times. How could Ciara sleep with another man? She shared her body with another man. I've never felt this before. It really hurt; all I can imagine is James all over her. The image is not pleasing; it is driving me insane.

Just this once, I understand what Hillary felt. Why would Ciara do this? One wrong situation and she throws us away and fucks another man. A man I had been begging her to end the relationship with.

I don't get it. My mind is a mess as I drove back to my apartment.

Ciara

Weeks had turned into months since Phillip stormed out. He has rightly made it known that he doesn't want to speak with me. Each time I try to talk to him about us, he finds a reason to hang up or say he's busy and has to go.

I cry myself to sleep every night because I miss him so much, and I don't know how to apologize for what I have done. The worst part was Hillary calling me a day after he left, begging for my forgiveness if she had caused a rift between us. She told the same story Philip had told me, including the fact she had returned the engagement ring.

I don't know how to reach out to Phillip after what I said to him. He won't talk to me; I see the hurt in his eyes. We are both hurting; it turns out he's more stubborn than I am.

Now, whenever he comes to pick up Filipa, he makes certain to wait outside my house. Today, however, he came in since Filipa was not ready yet. I left him in the living area while I went upstairs to get Filipa ready. By the time I came down with her, Philip's face was angry.

He held the ultrasound picture in front of me. "What is this? "He asked acidly.

"My ultrasound picture. I am pregnant," I state quietly.

"This just keeps getting fucking better," he scorns. "For a girl who once told me she couldn't get pregnant, you sure do get knocked up quick on first-night rolls in the hay; come on my darling Filipa let's go."

His words hit like a bitch-slap to the face.

"Bye Mommy."

I just nodded to my daughter as she walked out with her father, my eyes filled with tears. He didn't give me a chance to tell him he is the father.

My life keeps getting more and more complicated. Yesterday, James saw the same picture and thought it was my way of telling him he was going to be a father. He was super excited; he couldn't believe it. I didn't have the heart to tell him it's not his. I just smiled and played along.

Now, Phillip cannot even bear to get near me. He made a mistake by not telling me Hillary was in his apartment, and I made a mistake of getting drunk and ending up naked in bed with James. He does not realize his careless mistake drove me to drink that night.

When Phillip returned with Filipa, I tried to talk to him, but he just walked out on me, then texted me saying he will be traveling for two weeks, but that he will call Filipa just before her bedtime every night.

I cried myself to sleep again; my eyes were like waterfalls.

The next two weeks went by fast, not because I was having any fun. My head feels like it's buried in sand. The only thing I could do was work, but even that wasn't a walk in the park since James kept showering me with attention that I frankly didn't want.

I had to stick with professional contributions just so we could get through the day. I decided to only show up at work only when Steve was there or when James wasn't. My life just felt messy and chaotic. All I want is a simple life. Now mess is all a see with no path to clear the mess.

By the fifth week of my mess, I'd caught a terrible cold, which meant I had to be in bed. James and Steve were out of town. Stella was also not feeling well, and I didn't want to trouble my parents, so I stayed home.

Phillip stopped by to visit Filipa; he noticed how sick I looked. He decided to spend the night to help with Filipa, so I went straight to bed and left Filipa with him.

I woke up late the next morning feeling a bit better, only to be met with Phillip's irate face. Instantly, I felt worse. What could I have possibly done while sleeping?

"Your doctor's office just called saying they have called in the meds you can use. They said that it should help your cold and that it's safe during pregnancy." He pauses, almost as like he's trying to reign in his vexation.

His tone has me tongue-tied, and I contemplate whether I should fight or flight, but I am too weak to do either.

"Now my question to you is how the fuck is James the father if you are ten plus weeks, because, if I am correct six weeks ago was the first time you slept with him, unless you have been fucking him while you were fucking me," he lashed out. "If that's the case, I would say that either of us could be the father. I'm telling you right now, I want custody of my child, and I don't fucking care if you marry him. You will not withhold information about my child from me again. You will be hearing from my lawyers," he says before stomping out of my house for the umpteenth time.

My tears could not stop rolling as I watched him walk out again. He's never going to forgive me for sleeping with James. How did I get to this point? I wanted to run after him, but I could not bring myself to move. His words still played like a broken record in my head. Filipa brought me out of my trance when she giggled out loud as she watched her cartoon show.

Sixteen

Philip

Storming out seems like the easier solution these days. I can't stand the thought of looking at her and not being able to hold her or kiss her. It's killing me each time I see her, but she just keeps pushing me away.

First, I found out she's pregnant with James's child. How the fuck did that happen? I have been trying for months, and after one night with the jerk, she is pregnant. I mean, I could be the father, and she could try to keep me in the dark again. But why would she keep doing this?

James will not raise my child; it's bad enough I have to deal with him in Filipa's life. There is no way James is the father. I doubt Ciara was sleeping with him before now, but I must know for sure, so I am going to request a court ordered DNA test for the baby.

At least Hillary and I are on better terms now. I apologized to her for lashing out at her, and she gave me my ring back, but none of it matters now.

She also informed me she spoke with Ciara and told her the truth.

I just nodded when she said that.

"Don't give up on her so easily. You have something worth fighting for," she'd said to me. But right now, I feel like we have nothing but torn souls.

After days of moving around like a shell of myself, Henry finally asked, "Are you going to tell me what's going on with you, or do I need to get you drunk?"

I let out a sigh. "Ciara is pregnant." Henry's face lights up. "And I don't know if the baby is mine or that asshole she's engaged to." I managed to swipe his happy face to disbelief.

"What!?" I returned a sad chuckle. "I thought you had things worked out with her."

"I thought I did too, but who knew one mistake would make her throw us away and fuck another man?"

"I find it hard to believe that she would fuck another guy, fiancé or not. I met her, and I hung out with her. She may put up a front, but that woman is in love with you. Philip."

"I want to believe that too, but she told me herself what she did."

"Honestly, I don't believe it, but the question is, are you going to forgive her because you are no saint yourself?"

"I want to forgive, but I'm hurt. We had something special, that's why it hurt. I've fucked lots of women, but I've only ever made love with Ciara and the thought of her in bed with another man is like her looking me in the eye and stabbing me right in the heart."

"I'm sorry, man, but if you love her, you have to forgive her."

"I know, but it just hurts so bad, and each time I see her, I crave to hold her and inhale that honey and floral scent that I've missed so much. My mind plays the image of James doing the same and it just tears at my soul."

"I understand, but would you rather live without her or forgive and move past this mistake?"

I don't respond, but he's right. I would rather move past this and have Ciara than let her marry James.

"Let's drink. A little alcohol may help you work towards that forgiveness."

Seventeen

Ciara

I called Stella on FaceTime, and for the first time, I confessed everything to her. She looked at me, then burst into laughter.

"I am surprised it took you this long to finally confess. Just so you know, anyone standing next to you and Philip can put two and two together. Did you honestly think we couldn't tell?"

I nodded because I foolishly thought I was covering my tracks.

"Yeah, right," she laughs. "Ciara, dear, I know Philip is in town whenever you go out in the evening and don't come back till the next day. I bet you James knows too. He couldn't be that stupid."

"What do I do now, Stella? I need to let James know he's not the father of my child, and I need to fix things with Philip. I know we are both hurting. I thought I was stubborn, but he's worse. He won't even speak to me." I exhaled my frustration.

"I can't help you there; all I know is that Philip is still in love with you, and I don't think he will refuse to see you if you show up in LA."

"That's a good idea. I'll find out his schedule, then fly to LA. Thanks, Stella."

"You're welcome. So, how far along are you?"

"Three months. I can't wait to find out if it's a boy or girl," I stated.

"Mom and Dad are excited for you."

"I bet. They wished they could just get me to pick one man."

"They already know that your heart picks Philip; you just needed to say it out loud."

I called Philip's office after speaking with Stella, and his PA informed me he was in New York for the next three weeks and may not be back for a while. I thought about going to visit him in NY but decided to wait until his return. In three weeks, I would have found out the sex of the baby, anyway.

Three weeks went by so fast when all I did was work and take care of Filipa and myself. I stayed away from James. He didn't push either, which was great.

By the end of the three weeks, Philip informed me he would show up to see Filipa. I was so excited about him coming; I went the extra length to look good. Got my hair done, applied a full face of makeup, even put on a sexy dress to show off my little baby bump. I tried to stay calm when he pressed the bell.

I went to answer it, but jealousy washed over me like a tidal wave when I saw Philip with a petite brunette lady. She had on a sexy red dress hugging her figure, and her wavy hair was perfectly styled along with her flawless make-up. She was smiling brightly up at Philip.

"Hi," I managed to say.

"Hi, I hope you don't mind me stopping by with some-one," he says in a light tone.

"Hi Ciara, I am Ella. So sorry to stop by like this, but I wanted to meet Filipa and wouldn't let Philip talk me out of it, Maggie said she's adorable."

Before I could answer, Filipa raced into Philip's arms. I had wanted to turn them away before, but it was now too late; I let them in. The father and daughter reunion was too beautiful a sight.

I walked away to the bathroom to calm myself. How dare he show up with one of his dates to my house? I spent my day getting ready for someone that was busy having fun with another woman.

Who am I kidding? Philip has moved on from me, and the sooner I do the same, the better.

I couldn't hide in the bathroom forever. I went back to the living room and found Ella playing cheerfully with my daughter. I moved to the kitchen, busying myself with nothing.

Philip stepped away from them and came to me. "How are you, Ciara?"

"Very good, thank you, and you?"

"Good. How's the baby?"

"He's good."

"It's a boy!" he said, unable to hide his excitement.

"Yes," I replied stoically, though I almost cracked a smile. At the cheerful look on his face.

"When did you find out the sex of the baby?" The excitement in his voice was gone.

"Three days ago."

He looked hurt by my response, as though he thought I wasn't going to tell him. We stood staring at each other.

"You look very nice tonight."

"Thank you."

"Are you going on a date?"

I couldn't tell if it was just a casual ask, or if he really wanted to know. How dare he ask me that when he brought his own date to meet my daughter? How close could they be for him to introduce her to Filipa?

"I was going to, but it got canceled at the last minute." I couldn't let him think I got all dressed up for him.

He nodded, but I could see his anger subtly surface on his face. He turns away from me. "Ella, we need to get going," he says.

She hugs Filipa and comes to me.

"It's so nice to finally meet you, and Filipa is simply adorable."

"Thank you."

"I'll wait in the car Philip," she says as she leaves.

Philip hugs Filipa before heading to the door. Just before he walked out, he said, "My PA said you called while I was in New York. Was there something you wanted to discuss with me?"

"No, I hadn't heard from you in a while, and I just thought I'd check in to say hello."

"That's it? No other reason?"

"Should there be?"

He shook his head and left.

Once the door shut, I got Filipa ready for bed, changed into my PJs, and removed the make-up that I wasted all my time on. When is this going to end? I thought to myself. I could still feel our attraction, but he's with someone new.

I need to practice moving on.

Philip

I can't believe it. We are having a boy! I have no doubt in my mind that the baby is mine. But why would she not call and tell me about it? She didn't even care that I was with Ella.

She's all dressed up for a night out, too, probably with James. I am not sure how much longer I can take us like this. I've really missed her. I was excited when my PA told me she called, but then I see her, and she says nothing.

I thought it was a good idea to show up with Ella, my cousin, who just was in Chicago for an event and has been wanting to meet Ciara and Filipa. She thought Filipa was adorable, and that Ciara seemed nice. I didn't want to tell her more.

When we drove back to the city, I dropped Ella off at her event and went back to my hotel. Normally, I would have talked to Ciara all night, but I am not sure what to expect if I call her now. I can only find out and move forward with her by calling.

I picked up the phone and called her, and to my surprise, she answered.

"Hi, Philip."

"Hi, is Filipa ok?"

"She's good. I just put her to bed."

"Good..." Silence lingers. I can hear her breathing, and I bet she can hear me too.

"When did you find out the baby is a boy?"

"Three days ago."

"Were you ever going to tell me?" I anxiously asked.

"I called your office, but your PA said you were still in NY, so I waited till you got back. I was going to tell you when you came over, but..."

"Ciara, she's, my cousin. Ella is my cousin." I hear her exhale. I pause, letting that sink in. "I've missed you, Ciara," I confessed.

"Missed you too," she replied.

Relief washes over me, but I didn't know what else to say.

I've forgiven her like Henry advised, though it still hurts every time I remember it. I still believe the child is mine, but how do I bring up the topic without bringing us back to where we were?

"Are you certain the baby is a boy?"

"As certain as possible, unless the ultrasound is wrong."

"How've you been?"

"Pretty ok, keeping busy."

"That's good; I fly back to LA tomorrow, lots to do for the next couple of weeks."

"Busy is always a good thing, right? Keeps our mind away from other stuff."

"Yes, it is."

We ended up talking about many stuff; we sounded like our old selves again. Nevertheless, there are still things that need to be talked about urgently, but it can wait.

Ciara

Talking to Philip last night made me realize how much I've missed him. We spoke at length, catching up on months of silence. A few laughs made us feel better. He only hung up when he noticed the time, as he had to catch an early flight.

I decided, for me to move forward with Philip, I needed to close the door on James once and for all.

Just before I left home, I called James, letting him know we needed to talk. We met earlier than usual at the job site before Steve arrived.

I had every word planned out in my mind, and I arrived fifteen minutes early to prepare myself. I inhale and exhale to keep calm, realizing that breaking up with James isn't going to be as easy as I thought it would be. When James pulled up, I got out of my car and waited for him to walk up to me.

"Hi, James."

"Hi, Ciara." He pulled me into a hug and kissed me. I had to break away from the embrace before things got intense. I took a deep breath and then spit out the truth. "James, I am sorry, but we can't work out."

"Why?"

I looked him straight in the eye. "Because my heart belongs to another, and it would be unfair to keep this going," I firmly stated.

"Philip?" he asked, and I nodded. "Guess I was a fool in thinking what I saw between you two was all my imagination, and that you wearing my ring meant something," he forced himself to say.

"I honestly don't know what to say other than I am sorry. I really wanted us to work out, but my heart belongs to him, right from the moment I met him."

"The baby is Philip's child," he stated.

I gave no answer, but my silence spoke volumes.

His face changes immediately; I could see the anger engulfing him. He takes a deep breath. "How long have you been fucking him?"

"Please, let's not do this, James. Please take the ring back." I tried to give him the ring, but he knocked it out of my hand, and it fell to the ground.

"How long Ciara?" he yells.

"That's my business; I will not answer you, so take the ring back." I picked it up and tried giving it to him again.

"It is my business to know how long you were fucking him while wearing my ring."

I realize there's no getting through to him. I need to leave. Rather than trying to talk, I threw the ring at him and turned to walk away. Before I can leave, he pulls me back and shoves me to the car, yelling, "How long!"

Just then, I heard Steven's voice. "James, get the hell away from her. If you harm her, I will fucking hurt you."

James then takes a step back. He picks up the ring as I run into Steven's arms. "I don't want to be a rich boy's sloppy seconds, and I can't wait to see when he dumps you. I'll be sure to have a front-row laugh," he spits out as he gets into his car and drives off.

"So, my guess is you finally broke up with him?" Steven said.

All I could do was nod, resting my head on his chest; I was still shaken by James's attack.

"I am glad you finally did."

"Now, he hates me."

"He's just hurt. He'll get over it." Steven tells me to go home and rest, and that he will take care of the job today.

I returned home and called Philip.

He answers right away. "Ciara, are you ok?"

"Yes." I could hear background noise. "Are you in a meeting?"

"Yes, but I can talk. Is something wrong?"

"No," I lied.

"Ok, you can call me back later."

I decided not to tell Philip. He just might get upset enough to come and fight James.

"Are you sure?" he said.

"Yes, I am fine," I convincingly replied. "Ok, I'll call you back later." I hung up and went to relax and later picked up some design work to do.

Philip called me back later in the day, and we talked as we normally did. After we spoke, I decided I would surprise him in LA the next day.

I realized after all that had happened, Philip deserves to hear my apologies in person. Still, I am not sure how I present my apology to him and ask for forgiveness, but I need to do this. We have been in a good place lately, and we talk and laugh a lot; it would be a shame if my apology backfired.

I have no hotel plans and only one change of clothes. My intention is to beg for his forgiveness.

When I arrived at his office, his PA said he was in a meeting.

"Do you know how long the meeting might be?"

"It is scheduled for 2 hours, and they started half an hour ago."

"If the meeting ends ahead of time, please call me. I'll be in the café downstairs." Looks like I've extra time to practice my ask, I thought.

In the café, I placed my order and responded to a few emails. I suddenly realized Amy would throw a fit if I didn't call her. I immediately dialed her number. The line had just rung twice when I saw Philip dashing into the café. I hung up the call and got up. When he saw me, he pulled me into a tight hug.

"Are you ok? What's wrong?"

Panic is all over his face. "Nothing is wrong; I just wanted to talk to you in person." I state, my heart rate is elevated.

"Ok," he says with a cautionary expression.

My breathing slows down as we sat down across from each other.

"Is your meeting over?" I ask to control my mind and breathing.

"No, Lorraine came in and told me you're here and waiting here for me. I had the meeting rescheduled right away."

"You didn't have to do that. I could've waited."

"Don't worry about that. Tell me why you're here."

"I wanted to apologize to you for all that's happened. I returned James's ring to him a few days ago."

He stares at me, shocked, as he exhales and wipes his face. Runs his hand through his short dark hair.

"Also, the baby is yours. I found out two days before the whole situation with Hillary happened. I wanted to tell you in person, which is why I didn't tell you on the phone. I'm sorry everything happened the way it did. Can you find it in your heart to forgive me for what happened with James?" I ask pleadingly.

He looks at me quizzically but remains silent.

"Please say something," I plead, desperately hoping he would forgive me. But before I had a chance to say anything else, his lips were pressing against mine intensely.

When we break from the kiss, he mumbles, "We are having a son for real, Ciara?"

I laugh. "Yes, we are."

He pulls me into a hug and speaks gently into my ear, "I have missed you so much, and we are moving forward from here, agreed?" He pulls away from the hug to cup my face.

"Agreed," I answered back.

"Let's get back to my office." We went back to his office; he arranged my transportation to his apartment since he still had work to do.

While at his apartment, Amy called me back; she had just seen my missed call. I told her I was in LA, and Amy, being who she is, came over right away.

"Omg! you forgot to mention your obvious belly, dear," she exclaimed in the usual Amy fashion.

"I am sorry, a lot has been going on."

"I need all the details, and don't you dare leave anything out? Also, we are going out, and you're not allowed to say no or call Fancy Face."

I laugh. "Fancy Face?"

"Philip is Fancy Face, that's the name I am giving him, and I need to hear all about how he got you knocked up again, with a cocktail and no interference from him."

"Ok, but you realize when he gets back, and I am not here, he's going flip out on you," I state with a chuckle.

"He'll survive. I just don't need him disturbing our girls' night. Let's go. When he calls, we can tell him you're with me, but not where we are."

I didn't want to argue with Amy. "Can I at least leave him a note?"

"That you can do. We don't want him calling the police."

So, with Amy's permission, I left him a note saying: Out with Amy, will be back soon.

At the bar, Amy's cocktail got her tipsy as I filled her in on all that's happened. She was laughing at how I went from getting stuck in one relationship to a two-man love fiasco.

"Hey, aren't you glad I found my way out?" I said.

"Girl, you found your way out when you had that one-night stand with Fancy Face. I knew you were done for when you danced all night with him at Claire's wedding. Didn't you see the pictures I sent to you? You just didn't want to admit how badly you fell for him, but I am glad you corrected it all before it got out of hand."

"Thanks."

"So, are you going to move back to LA?"

"I really don't want to. My family is in Chicago, and you know I get lots of help from them. Besides, his mom hates me, and that's not encouraging."

"I can understand that, but you can't hold that against him."

"I know. I admit I love him, but I'm not sure about moving back here for him yet."

"Stop analyzing everything Ciara, I know that's what you do best, but just this once, let love guide you."

"I'll try," I say.

She stares me down.

"I promise to try," I respond. We continued our chat for a while. I don't even know how long, but suddenly, I see Philip approach us, pull up a chair, and sit right beside me.

He looked upset. I should have known even a note would upset him. "Ciara, where is your phone?"

"It's right here." I say as I dig it out of my bag and notice over 40 missed calls from him. My jaw dropped. I know I didn't turn my ringer off, so I turned my face to Amy.

Amy sighed. "Fine, I did it because I knew he would disrupt our time together; he always does that," she said, persuasively turning the guilty look to Philip.

I then turned to him. "Alright, but you have had your time. Can I take her home now?" he replies to her accusation.

"See, exactly what I said he would do."

They are both acting like children, but I can't help but be happy with the love they have for me. I turn to Amy and say, "Honestly, I was about to head back anyway because I need to rest, not because he came charging in here like a raging bull." I give him a threatening look.

"How about we meet tomorrow for brunch before I head to the airport?"

"Sounds good. I'll call you and let you know where. Please do rest and don't forget what we talked about." She gives me a hug and leaves.

"Are you ready to go?" Philip asks.

"How did you find us? I didn't leave that in the note."

"Amy's social media. She'd posted pictures of where she was, so it was easy to find you from there."

"And you just had to come here, didn't you?"

"Well, I got home, and you weren't there, only the note, and I called and called with no answer. I thought something happened to you."

"Am I to assume you called Amy as well?"

He nodded.

"You can't possibly think she's setting me up, do you? Not with my noticeable belly."

"I had that area covered. I was just worried."

"Ok, anyway, let's go."

We got up and headed for the door.

"You know you're not leaving tomorrow, right?" he states.

"Why not?"

"Do I need to spell it out for you?"

"Um, yes, because I have pregnancy brain."

"Well, I haven't had you naked in weeks, and you and I both know what that means."

Needless to say, I spent five days in LA before going back to Chicago. Philip and I talked about everything. The one thing we couldn't agree on is my hesitancy to move to LA because of his mom's outright dislike of me. We couldn't resolve that in just five days, so we'll discuss that more after the baby is born. In the meantime, we agreed wholeheartedly that we were both in love with each other.

Eighteen

Philip

"Ciara, please wake up. I need you. I can't go on without you. Please, my darling, wake up. I love you so much. Please wake up. Our son Carter is alive and well. He needs you, Filipa needs you, and I need you. Please, my love, wake up." I sat there watching her lie almost lifeless.

"Philip, you need to rest too. I will stay and watch her," Ciara's mom said to me.

"I can't. I need to stay here with her. If you don't mind, please."

"No, she's sleeping, and you look exhausted. I will stay with her and call you once she wakes up."

"Thank you, but I will wait right here."

"Ok then, I will get you a blanket and something warm to drink."

As she walked out, I sat there staring at Ciara sleeping, not moving, with all the machines beeping. Please wake up, Ciara. I really need you to wake up.

My thought wanders back to the last three days; I was in a meeting with my dad when she called me.

"Hi Ciara."

Her hysterical cry hit me right away. "Philip, I am so sorry to disturb you," she said through her sobs. "I can't believe he would do this to me."

"Are you okay? And who did what to you?"

"James. I can't believe he would do this to me; I went to his place to confront him about some work issues. He had changed the design without discussing it with Steven or me. The changes will set us back on cost and time." She went on telling me how her intention was to just discuss those changes, but James ended up throwing insults and lots of hurtful words at her.

More sobs spilled on the phone. She was driving and apologizing about all that had happened. I heard the horrid sound of screeching tires, a crash, and then her nearly lifeless groans of pain.

I have never felt as helpless as I did that day. I turned to my dad, who was watching as I yelled her name into the phone.

My father shook me into reality. "What's wrong?" He kept asking, but I was in no state to respond.

I called Stella immediately and told her Ciara had just left James's house and was probably in a car accident, then asked her to call an ambulance. I begged her to call me back as soon as she had updates.

Thirty minutes later, my phone rang as I paced my office. It was Stella, crying. She said Ciara is badly hurt; they are not sure if she or the baby will survive. I told her I was on my way. As soon as I hung up, I burst into tears as I turned to my dad.

"She's in terrible condition; they said she and the baby might not make it."

With panic in his eyes, my father arranged a private charter to get us to Chicago immediately. The four-hour flight felt like a lifetime as I called Stella mid-air to get an update on Ciara's status. She informed me Carter was delivered prematurely through an emergency C-section and seemed to be healthy. Ciara was still in surgery, and they were waiting.

I sat there, dazed. I vaguely heard my father saying, "Son, you have to be strong; she will pull through." By the time we landed in Chicago and arrived at the hospital, I broke down when I saw all the tubes attached to Ciara. Nothing in my thirty-two years could have ever prepared me for such a moment. I fell to her side and begged her to wake up.

Three days later, here I am still holding her hand with my own swollen knuckles from when I repeatedly punched

James when he visited. I blamed him for Ciara's accident. Had he not been so cruel to her, she wouldn't have become so distressed while driving.

Granted, he was hurt, but she's obviously pregnant and fragile. His attack on her was uncalled for. Then he strolls in, asking how she was doing. I attacked him without thinking. I launched all the rage I felt at him.

Now, the doctors' said Ciara is improving; her vitals were stable. All she needed to do was wake up. They assured me she would, but I sat there watching her. I prayed like I had never prayed in my life for her to wake up.

On the morning of the fourth day, I finally adhered to her parents' request to go shower, eat, and return. But just as I finished eating, they called me to tell me that Ciara had woken up and was asking for me.

I dashed to the hospital so fast. How I got there was a blur. When I got to her room, I found her in a sitting position with Carter in her arms and Filipa by her side. I rushed to her other side and pulled them all into a hug. Tears of joy filled my eyes as I kissed each forehead.

"I am so sorry, Phillip."

"Shh, not now. I am just so happy you are awake."

"Thank you for staying by my side; I was told you had been here the last three days."

"I couldn't leave, but your mom threatened to pull my visitation rights if I didn't go and shower."

She laughs. "Yeah, she told me."

Her mom came in and started speaking before I could respond. "Phillip, there you are, and aren't you a pleasant sight now? I will take the children so you two can talk."

We thanked her and handed our children over to her. As soon as the door shut behind her, Ciara and I deeply embraced each other.

"I am so sorry if I scared you," she whispered weakly.

"I don't know what I would have done without you being there for our children."

"I am sorry for all the pain I caused; I was just so confused."

"I know Ciara, we have a second chance; the question is, what do we do?

"Whatever you want is fine with me, Philip. I would move back to LA if that is what you want."

"All I want is you and our children and for us to have every legal, emotional, and spiritual right to each other."

"Done," she said.

I broke away from the embrace.

"So, you will marry me?"

"Yes, but I would need a better proposal than that."

"Yes, I can certainly manage a better one." I pulled her into another hug as she sobbed. "My darling, please tell me you're crying tears of joy."

"I am," she mumbled. "Philip, I have a confession to make. Steven told me I hadn't had sex with James since I was too knocked out to have sex. Unless James raped me, which I don't think he did. What he did, though, was take me to his house and undress me. When I woke up naked in his bed, I just assumed that I probably had sex with him. I really had no recollection of what happened, but it seems he wanted to punish me for leading him on. He decided not to correct my assumption and fueled my hurt by pushing for us to marry the next morning." She sighs.

"Per Steven, while I was drinking my hurt away, I had made a series of confessions about you and me having sex and how I was, and am, in love with you. Steven said he'd told James that it was all lies, that I was just drunk and all that was gibberish. James had asked Steven if he was aware of the situation, but luckily Steven wasn't, since I had never told him, which made Steven upset. When he found out.

"Since it was all gibberish, what changed?"

"Just before I fell asleep, I'd said to him I love Philip so much and he really hurt me today. That got him thinking about extending our hurt because he felt I'd made a fool of him."

"How did you find out about all this?"

"I went to his place to talk about work, but he told me how trashy I am, and that it's a good thing he didn't touch sloppy seconds like me. I asked him what he meant by that. He then said, "What do you think? I don't sleep with drunk sloppy seconds, especially when I can tell Mr. Nice Guy is about to drop your sorry ass." He let me think I had slept with him and even got excited about a baby that wasn't his; I guess he felt really betrayed and wanted to punish me."

She continued. "Once I stormed out of his house, I called Steven, and he told me his side of the story. Then I called you."

"It's all behind us now, and we need to plan our lives together. Will you really be happy in LA?"

"I'll be happy anywhere, as long as you're there with us."

"Oh, thank God. Because I really dread the Chicago winter weather," I laugh.

"I'll just have to open another office in LA or sell this business. For now, the focus is the children."

"For real, we are getting married."

"Yes, we are. I am so happy."

Thank you for reading The Red Eye

Please do leave me a review, I would like to read your review.

Please check out my other books

Tola and Kyle Forces of Destiny an enemies-to-lovers forbidden romance.

https://tinyurl.com/mpkf53wd

Tamara and Omar. Falsified A second chance steamy romance

https://tinyurl.com/mrxx9t58

Lande and Tate in Collide and an age gap romance

https://tinyurl.com/2t2e74j6

Connect with me.

I would love to hear from you.

Your reviews and thoughts, even a book recommendation is welcome.

I'm a reader too and enjoy good reads.

IG: https://www.instagram.com/a_akinosho/

Facebook:

https://www.facebook.com/authora.akinosho

Website http://www.authoraakinosho.com/

Printed in Great Britain
by Amazon

44445318R00118